Extra Galaxia
Science Agents #1

Pierre V. Comtois

Published by Rogue Phoenix Press, LLP
Copyright © 2019

ISBN: 978-1-62420-446-3

Credits
Cover Artist: Designs by Ms G
Editor: Sherry Derr-Wille

Acknowledgement

Thanks go out to Gregorio Montejo for ideas and tech support.

Chapter One

Plans Go Astray

"Rise and shine, you lovebirds!" called Finley in a voice deliberately calculated to drive Jules Santros crazy.

Hard rapping on the cabin door.

"You guys in there?" asked Finley, no doubt with a smirk on his face. "Honeymoon's over and ole Sol's waiting. We'll be in Mars orbit in three standard hours."

Jules tossed off the thin bed sheet and rolled from the bunk, inadvertently leaving Joan to shiver in the cool, air-conditioned cabin.

"Hey, buster." she said, grabbing for the sheet. "It's positively frigid in here."

"Who's frigid?" asked Finley from the other side of the door.

Growling, Jules staggered across the small cabin and hit the door controls. The panel slid open a crack, just enough to reveal Finley leaping away and out of reach.

"Can't a man and his wife get some sleep around here?" asked Jules in mock seriousness.

"Oh, is that what you were doing? Shucks. Thought I was interrupting something."

"You still smarting from that time I caught you and Pris—?

"Don't start that again. And don't you dare breath a word about it to those rumor mongers at Marsport!"

"Then go away and stop bothering us."

"Tell Pris we'll be out in twenty minutes, Finley," called Joan from where she still huddled in the bunk.

"Thanks, Joan. At least someone around here is taking things seriously."

"Get lost, you spoiler," said Jules, hitting the control button.

The door panel barely slid closed before he was back under the covers and reaching for his wife.

"Hey, didn't you hear Finley? We're wanted on deck."

"You told him twenty minutes," protested Jules, pulling Joan close.

"Well, it's going to take most of that time for me to get presentable."

"Then you'd better get a move on," replied Jules playfully, throwing off the sheet for the second time and herding Joan out of the bunk by way of a slap on her bottom.

~ * ~

Precisely twenty minutes later, Joan stepped into the control deck where Pris Gower sat in the navigator's chair. Across the confined space, grown suddenly more crowded with the appearance of the extra crew member, Finley was doing something over at the atmospherics panel.

It did not escape Joan's notice.

"So, it was you brought down the temp in our cabin." she said, propping her fists on her hips.

"I cannot tell a lie," confessed Finley, slinking back to the pilot's position.

"I can't believe he still thinks that's funny," said Joan looking over at Pris. "It was freezing in there last sleep period. I couldn't keep Jules away from me the whole time."

Pris shrugged. "Men. They never grow up."

"C'mon, Pris. With only a few hours left till we reach Mars, there won't be time to have any fun before this mission is officially over."

Joan softened. It was true. Six months ago, the Interplanetary Geological Survey teamed up she and Jules with fellow husband and wife team Finley and Pris Gower, pilot and navigator of the deep space survey ship *E.R. Burroughs* to explore a chain of worlds in the Cygnus system. As a xeno-geologist, Joan was more than excited when they came across Cygnus Alpha 12, a planet completely covered by a sea of liquid methane.

At the very least, it promised quite a diversity of life forms in such an unusual environment. She didn't know how diverse until she and Jules stumbled across a downed Coalition warship with some troopers still alive and determined to kill them. They'd managed to turn the tables on the troopers only to find out that the crashed ship had used some kind of dangerous new black hole technology Jules recognized as something the Consortium had experimented with and decided not to pursue.

It'd been touch and go for a while there as the still active forbidden tech threatened to get out of control...Jules even said it endangered all space-time. Joan wasn't sure about that but was sufficiently frightened by the experience to be relieved when they returned to their friends aboard ship. After their return, she filed her report with the Survey and thought that would be the end of it. She'd almost forgotten that Jules retired from Military Intelligence and old habits die hard. As it turned out, he'd filed his own report to former colleagues and whatever he wrote must have set off alarm bells because the next thing they knew, the *E.R. Burroughs* had been ordered to cancel the remainder of its tour and return to Mars immediately.

"What's our ETA, Pris?" asked Jules, appearing in the control room hatchway.

"Just under two point forty hours," replied Pris. "Have to admit, you guys can be pretty efficient when you want to be."

"I only need five minutes, it's Joan who takes up all the time," said Jules with a wink.

"I could cut that time in half if I didn't have to constantly fight off your advances," said Joan, punching Jules in the stomach with her fist.

"Ouch," laughed Finley from where he was scaling down the boosters.

"That message we received to turn back sounded serious," said Pris without turning her attention from the instruments. The approach to Mars with its two moons was tricky even for the best navigators.

Jules recognized the note of curiosity in the statement and was genuinely sorry he couldn't fill in she and Finley more than what they already knew...which was not much. He'd warned Joan to say as little as possible about what happened on Cygnus Alpha 12. Knowing they'd have to tell their partners something, they told them about the downed ship and the attack by the troopers, including their escape from them. Nothing about the black hole tech or the near catastrophe that had faced the entire galaxy that he'd barely averted.

"Military Intelligence takes everything seriously," replied Jules cautiously. "We did find a Coalition ship after all. You can't blame them for wanting to know all about it."

"Think they'll be sending a salvage operation to recover the wreck?" asked Finley.

"Possibly...or a demo team."

"Wonder how it ended up way out there in the first place?"

"Your guess is as good as mine. Up to no good, that's for sure."

The Terran Consortium had been at war with the Outer Arm Coalition off and on for over fifty Earth years, having come in contact with it when a survey vehicle similar to the *E.R. Burroughs* encountered an advanced colony of a subject people deep in the newly discovered Atullun Nexus. It was fired upon without any warning and managed to limp back to Altair IV with the story. After that, the Consortium dispatched a task force to the Nexus to chastise the colony but ended up tangling with a Coalition battle fleet instead. Luckily, the enemy had no idea of the power of Mark IX photon pulse cannons and had the worst of the fight. It was not to be the last anyone heard of them. The war was one marked by a number of deep space skirmishes and full-scale battles numbering over a dozen in the decades since with neither side getting the upper hand. And though Consortium strategists had no doubt that they would end up the ultimate victor, it was not going to be a cake walk.

Time passed all too quickly until finally the *E.R. Burroughs* received clearance from Marsport and Pris calculated a course that would take the ship in by Deimos before slinging around to the planet's equator. From there, it was a simple affair for the experienced Finley to cut the boosters and allow the ship to slowly descend, using Mars' thin atmosphere as a brake.

"What it amounts to is a controlled fall," explained Finley as atmospheric condensation streaked the forward view ports. Suddenly, the wispy cloud formations gave way and the red and pink soil of the dusty planet loomed ahead of them.

As the ship continued to slacken speed by use of its belly thrusters, the green of cultivated areas, irrigated by waters located beneath the poles, came into view. In another few minutes they came within sight of Marsport, its multiple bubble domes gleaming in the weak sunlight.

Finley pulled back on the cyclical and the *E.R. Burroughs* pulled up, coming to a hovering stop over a scorched landing pad. In a matter of seconds, he had the survey ship on solid ground and cut the whine of the thrusters.

"Welcome to Marsport," he said.

Chapter Two

Trouble

"What?"

"I said," repeated Joan, removing the oxygen mask from her face, "it's going to feel good to be home again, even if the mission was cut short."

"Oh," said Jules, fixing a mask to his own face and breathing deep. Although terraforming had begun almost three hundred years ago, Mars was far from a completely comfortable place for people to live. The atmosphere, for instance, was still pretty thin with a relatively low oxygen content. Thus, for anyone venturing outside, there was still the need to saturate their lungs with pure oxygen first, followed by the use of the occasional oxygen-tube between times.

Jules and Joan bid goodbye to Finley and Pris amid hugs and handshakes before going their separate ways. A temporary situation to be sure as Joan was scheduled to meet with the Gowers again in a few days for debriefing by Survey officials. Jules was excused due to having his own appointment with Military Intelligence in a couple hours. Just enough time to escort Joan to their living unit under dome three before setting off.

Leaving the government terminal, they boarded a public speedcar that raced along reserved lanes to dome three covering the two point eight mile distance in minutes. Without the need to step outside, the couple entered the spacious lobby crowded with people coming and going and stepped into an up capsule. The ride was only a few flights, there not being that many tall buildings in Martian cities, so they soon found themselves at the door to Suite 436. Joan dug out her laser-key from somewhere and signaled the door it was all right to let them in.

Inside was well lit with a wide bank of clear plas windows giving a view over dome three and the nearby Martian landscape outside. It was a beautiful day.

"I didn't realize how tired I was," said Joan, throwing herself on the sofa.

"Count your blessings," replied Jules, checking to see what was available in the 'fridge. "I have to dash over to headquarters in a few minutes."

"Tell Director Leclerc he should be more thoughtful."

"Right," laughed Jules, picking out a Coke and wasting no time unsealing the vacuum pack and taking a long slug.

"Well, don't forget to take some 'tubes with you," reminded Joan. "Remember, you're not aboard ship anymore."

"I'll grab some now," said Jules, crossing the room and taking a few sticks from a dispenser. "Well, no use putting it off, I guess."

Joan accompanied him to the door and kissed him goodbye.

"Be back in a few hours," said Jules, slipping out the door.

"Bye."

Jules wasted no time descending to the lobby and hailing a speedcar. The drive took him out of dome three, through seven and twelve, around a stony outcropping that divided the northern and southern dome clusters, and into dome one where all the government offices were located.

There, the speedcar came to a halt in the lobby of a non-descript square block of a building that sported no placards or any other designation as to what its purpose was but it didn't matter, everyone knew what went on inside those blank, white walls.

Ahead of schedule, Jules took his time heading to an up capsule that took him to the top floor of the windowless structure. Stepping out into a quiet corridor, he stood a moment, taking it in. The synth-carpeting beneath his feet, the stereopticals of pastoral scenes on Earth, the iso-walls he knew were lined with the most advanced detection-search devices known to man, even the plas-glass partition at the end of the hall were all familiar to him. In a previous life, before joining the Interplanetary Geological Survey, Jules had been a secret agent. Well, not exactly an agent, just an engineer in the Military Intelligence Science Division where he spent ten years retro-engineering alien tech. It was something he grew tired of eventually and requested out. It was then he joined Joan with the Survey. He'd thought he'd seen the last of these featureless hallways and the labs on the floors below, deep beneath the Martian surface, but he had a feeling that he hadn't.

Taking a drag from one of his oxygen-tubes, Jules headed for the plas-glass partition and entered officer country; more specifically, the office of Henri Leclerc, director of MI, or Military Intelligence. It used to be General Leclerc but now it was just plain director, but that was enough.

Knowing he'd been checked over every which way from Sunday by the devices hidden within the iso-walls, he made his way from the up capsule to the partition where he announced himself to the woman occupying a work station in the center of the otherwise featureless room.

"Go right in, Mr. Santros," she said, "the director is waiting for you."

"Thanks."

Past the final door, he entered another office, this one twice as big as the secretary's and equally as featureless except for the X-ray plas windows banked behind the director's workstation. Jules knew that from outside the building, the featureless walls showed nothing but blank stone. From inside, however, the nature of the X-ray plas windows allowed a view outside. Just now, the view looked over green farm land beyond the dome that stretched out to the horizon where a pinkish haze indicated that a soil redactor was working, slowly nutrisizing the Martian sands in advance of seeding operations. Still somewhat cold outside for successful planting of most Earthly crops, terraforming had still managed to make the Martian climate hospitable enough for some varieties of winter wheat and other genetically altered vegetables and varieties of ground nuts. It was enough to make farming on Mars worthwhile and even profitable.

"Have a seat, Jules," said the man behind the workstation, which was what people in another century might have referred to as a desk except it was now far more than that.

Leclerc had risen in welcome to Jules, his big frame dwarfed somewhat behind the expansive workstation.

"How's Joan?" asked Leclerc, after he'd retaken his own chair.

"Good. Thanks for asking," said Jules, sucking on a 'tube.

"Nothing different around here I see."

"Nope. Still the same routine."

"How goes the war?"

"You watch the 'casts, don't you?"

"Sure."

"So, you know how it's going. Pretty much stalemate at the moment."

"That incident out at Procyon hasn't rattled anyone?"

"You know it has and before you point it out, no, that wasn't in the 'casts. Officially, we were jumped by Coalition forces, but we managed to fight them off before they could do any harm to our colonies."

"Ambushed, you mean."

"All right, ambushed. How they were able to take us so completely by surprise had strategists in Command scrambling and people here wondering where the ax of blame was going to fall until your report came in."

"As I reported, it was black hole tech," confirmed Jules. "A variation of the kind we were working on but basically the same theory."

"We'd wondered how they managed to take us by surprise."

In his report, Jules described how he and Joan discovered a downed Coalition vessel that appeared to be emanating time distortion effects. Years before, Jules had been lead engineer for Military Intelligence, reverse engineering black hole technology acquired from the Coalition. That line of research was quickly abandoned when it became apparent the slightest damage to the containment unit harnessing the artificial black hole could result in a temporal rift. An effect that had the potential of engulfing the entire galaxy, wiping out all reality. No one knew exactly what that would mean, but there were theories. Time could be bent, twisted, mixed, the immutable laws of nature would become elastic and unpredictable. In short, it was deemed by everyone concerned that the research was too dangerous to pursue and the whole effort was shut down. That being the case, how do you put the genie back in the bottle? The Coalition already had the tech and if their military situation disintegrated enough, the temptation would grow to risk using it to regain the upper hand. Because the bottom line was, black hole tech, as dangerous as it was, bypassed time and granted faster than light speed. Something no general could ignore. With it, a fleet of warships say, could get the jump on an opposing force anytime, anywhere. Which was exactly what Jules confirmed in his report. The Coalition had not only found a way to harness a temporal black hole but had installed it in at least some of their warships. The only problem was that like Earth's Military Intelligence, they failed to find a way to properly secure the artificial black hole. A hit by a Terran warship that disabled one of those vessels, forced it down on Cygnus Alpha 12 where he and Joan found it. It was only luck that Jules was able fix the problem then. There was no guarantee that next time, and there *would* be a next time if the Coalition persisted in using the technology, there would be anyone else on hand who knew how to do the same thing.

"It was the same tech as we worked on thirteen years ago," pointed out Jules, after a moment of thought. "Only then, we called it 'director mechanics for deep space navigation'."

"I thought it was an effective code name, whatever it meant."

"It wasn't intended to mean anything," said Jules. "Did they see through it? Any chance they got the tech from us?"

"Spies, you mean? We considered that but dismissed it. We got the basic science from them after all. They were way ahead of us at the time. After we shut down your unit, why would they bother trying to get anything from us?"

"Do you think the Coalition is doing this strictly on their own?"

"Right. One consolation is that their military position must be more precarious than we figured for them to resort to such dangerous methods as black hole tech."

"It does confer on them massive advantages," said Jules. "Why, a Coalition fleet could show up in Earth orbit even as we speak."

"Then you understand the gravity of the situation." Leclerc smiled, aware of the pun.

Jules quietly shook his head and took a drag on his 'tube. Outside, a lone flyer scudded along far off in the pink sky.

"Anyway, to come to the point, that's why I asked that you report to me right away."

"Joan wasn't very happy about that. You interrupted her survey mission."

"She'll get over it. If she wants to go on other missions, we're going to have to do something about this black hole business."

"Meaning?"

"Meaning we want to take you on again on a temporary basis, Jules."

"What for? You have the reverse engineering unit's original report as well as the one I just filed..."

"We do but that's not enough. Look, Jules. As soon as we received your report, we briefed the Prime Minister and seeing the danger, he had the Exterior Minister get in touch with the Coalition through channels. It seems they're as nervous as we are about the tech and agreed to a secret meeting at a neutral site to discuss the situation. There's a good chance we can negotiate this thing away, outlaw black hole tech and restore the balance of power."

"That's great, but what do you want me for?"

"Besides having worked on the tech before, you've just saved nearly the whole blamed universe, Jules. That makes you our expert on black hole tech whether you like it or not."

"I get it. You want to make me an adviser to the negotiating team?"

"Now you're cooking. There's no time to waste. You're leaving thirteen hundred hours day after tomorrow, Mars time on a naval shuttle. It'll rendezvous with Task Force 8 where you'll join the diplomatic team. You'll find out where the meeting is going to take place once you've transshipped. I don't have to tell you how important it is that we reach an agreement with the Coalition on this, do I?"

"Believe me, director, no one knows that better than I do."

Chapter Three

Threat Singular

In slow orbit around Cygnus 12, the *Corpus Cristi* had every right to believe it would be able to conduct its business without interference from Coalition forces.

Ordered into the neighborhood by Naval Headquarters, its orders were to locate a downed enemy vessel and recover it for further study by Military Intelligence. Easier said than done, considering the fact that the wreck contained an artificial black hole.

No doubt the brain boys in the Science Division were itching to reverse engineer the damned thing, thought Captain Stellis from his perch on the command deck. Something he couldn't blame them for in the least.

The nature of space warfare, what with its photon pulse guns, molecular borers, targeted lasers, and whatnot, was such that it was rare to find anything intact worth studying. In fact, it had never happened so far as he knew. Only now, there was an intact Coalition warship resting at the bottom of Cygnus 12's methane sea and by God, if there was any way to recover it, he was going to be the one to do it.

"Sir, recovery team confirms the target is intact and retains hull integrity," reported the XO. "Unless there are orders to the contrary, they intend to proceed as planned."

"Acknowledged," replied Stellis, watching the team's progress on an overhead monitor. It wouldn't be easy operating in liquid methane. Extreme caution had to be maintained at all times requiring slow, deliberate moves overseen by an alert supervisor. Stellis had confidence in Lt. Envers, an expert out of the Naval Academy's hostile environments school. He'd led teams in plenty of situations like this in the past. In fact, the *Corpus Cristi* had become the go to vessel whenever the Navy had a ticklish recovery problem to handle. Whether it was debris from enemy ships, retrieval of sensitive equipment, rescue of stranded crewmen, or recovery of bodies, the *Corpus Cristi* was called up. At first, Stellis resented the assignments as beneath his training as a combat officer, but gradually, he'd grown to accept the role, even take pride in it as a particular specialty that no other ship in the Consortium was trained to do. Maybe next time he saw Admiral Jorly, he'd suggest the design of a new patch for the *Cristi*'s uniforms—

Suddenly, Stellis' reverie was shattered by the sound of emergency klaxons filling the *Cristi*'s insides.

"What the hell?"

"Long range sensors detect a ship entering the system, sir," reported the XO.

"Identify," barked Stellis calling up his local screens.

"Signals indicate it's a Coalition cruiser, sir."

"Delta class," added the sensor officer.

"A light cruiser then," mused Stellis. *No heavy weapons, so that's good.*

When it was still tasked as part of a battle group, the *Cristi* was classed as an up armored destroyer and still possessed the pulse cannons and targeted lasers to prove it. If push came to shove, it could handle the Coalition cruiser.

"Any consorts?"

"Nothing yet, sir. Wait, there *are* more. Looks like a Strike Group."

"Positions."

"Wait one."

What was a Coalition Strike Group doing here? Stellis wondered. *A coincidence? Not likely.*

"Damn," he said aloud. "Headquarters assured us no one would know about this mission or about that ship down there."

"Intelligence has been known to be wrong before," reminded the XO.

"Sir," said the sensor officer, "The light cruiser is well in the lead. The rest of the Strike Force is lagging behind."

"Red alert, combat stations. I think we've got a fight on our hands, boys."

Again, the klaxon sounded, this time with more urgency as the one hundred and eighty-two crew members of the *Corpus Cristi* scrambled to duty stations and weapons were powered up.

"Mr. Urutu, break orbit and assume attack position," commanded Stellis.

"Aye, sir."

A sustained burn from the port thrusters lifted the *Cristi* away from the pull of Cygnus 12 and pointed its bow toward the approaching enemy.

"XO, order Lt. Envers to demo the enemy wreck and get his team topside in triple hurry," ordered Stellis.

"Aye, sir. The shuttle is already powering up for quick assent."

"We'll hold off the enemy force as long as we can, but Envers needs to get back as fast as possible."

"Sir, ship is battle secure," reported the Weapons Officer.

"Acknowledged. Sparks, any communication from the enemy force?"

"Wait one. Nothing. Shall we hail?"

"What the hell. Maybe we can stall them some. Send standard hail."

"Hailing."

There were a few moments of silence as Stellis watched the diving team leave the sunken wreck and head back to the surface of the methane sea. By his calculations, it would take them about a half hour to reach the shuttle where it floated on the surface. After that, only a few minutes more for the shuttle to reach orbit where it could be picked up by the *Cristi*.

Hopefully, the link up would not have to be made under fire, thought Stellis.

"Sir, enemy cruiser is returning our hail," said Sparks.

"Open frequency." Stellis paused then "This is Captain Nathaneal Stellis of the Terran Consortium destroyer *Corpus Cristi*. Who am I speaking to?"

Stellis was conscious about keeping his naturally aggressive nature in check. The immediate object here was to stall for time. He glanced at the monitor showing Lt. Envers' progress and was relieved to see he was making good time to the surface.

"I am Sanbooglaphno, Imajo of the Coalition..." the ship's translating computer had difficulty keeping up with the officer's introduction, the usual problem encountered with the mix of languages used by the Coalition forces. *It didn't matter who was aboard the other ship anyway, only their intentions,* thought Stellis.

"...demand that you stand down and leave this sector immediately," Sanbooglaphno was saying.

"This sector is unclaimed by either the Coalition or the Consortium and has been considered free range by agreement made at the interstellar conference of 2402. We are on a peaceful mission involving scientific research and have no intention of leaving until it is concluded."

"Do not bandy words with me, Captain," replied Sanbooglaphno. "I am well aware of your mission to retrieve a damaged Coalition war vessel that has crashed on Cygnus 12. Again, I order you to leave this sector. There will be no further warning."

"He's cut off communication, sir," said Sparks.

"Damn, so they do know about the crashed ship," declared Stellis. *If I were in their position, I wouldn't be inclined to let it fall into the hands of the enemy either.*

"Sir," said the XO. "Lt. Envers has reached the shuttle."

"Good, I..."

BLANG!

The *Corpus Cristi* shook under the impact of pulse cannon fired at long range.

"Firing at us without warning," cried Urutu.

"At least that commander was as good as his word," noted the XO.

"Weapons Officer, return fire, bow lasers," shouted Stellis. "Target the light cruiser."

"Lasers targeted and fired, sir."

That should compel evasive action, keeping it too busy to shoot back, thought Stellis. *If only its escorts would hang back another few minutes.*

"Mr. Urutu, bring port guns to bear."

"Aye, sir."

Stellis followed the action on his monitors as the *Corpus Cristi* turned about to bring as many of its guns into play as possible. While the ship was still maneuvering, an ion boring beam shot from the enemy vessel and passed through the area of space where *Cristi* had been before it began its turn.

"Port weapons units, prepare to fire," said Stellis.

"Ready, sir."

"Enemy vessel painted and targeted."

"Fire full broadside," ordered Stellis, gripping the arms of his command chair.

Even as a full spread of impulse beams lanced from the ship's recessed gun emplacements, the XO informed Stellis the shuttle was coming up from the planet's surface at full burn. Without awaiting orders, Lt. Envers remotely ignited the nucleo-demolition charges placed beneath the enemy wreck. All that indicated the charges were successful was a huge plume of liquid methane that boiled into the green skies of Cygnus 12 over the place where the Coalition wreck once rested. In seconds, it receded again as the sea for miles around collapsed inward. Somewhere below, the sea floor gave way and the Coalition wreck, along with its dangerous artificial black hole, was buried under tons of rock and silt.

Buried forever, thought Stellis hopefully.

"Estimated time to link up is four minutes," called out the XO.

"Very well," said Stellis, keeping track of the enemy cruiser which was now halted dead in space. The escorts had slowed. "WO, did that last salvo put the fear of God into those Coalition bastards?"

"Seems so, sir. Forward motion has stopped and there's some damage to its control surfaces. I think we hit the command hut, Captain." The WO could not help a slight smile from creasing his lips.

"Very good, weapons. Extend my congratulations to the gunners."

"Aye, sir."

Stellis could imagine the conditions aboard the enemy craft if that last broadside raked its bridge. It should have knocked the fight out of it for sure. The cost of overconfidence on the part of Sanbooglaphno or whatever he called himself. He should have waited for his escorts.

There was nothing wrong with the cruiser's engines however, so with the demolition of the wreck on Cygnus 12, Stellis judged his mission was completed.

"Time to get out of here, Mr. Urutu. Plot a course back to Sol."

"Aye, sir."

"XO, what about that shuttle?"

"Entering aft hangar now sir...tethers secured, magniclamps in place. All hands reported safe and sound."

"Good, close hangar doors and let's get out of here."

"Shuttle secure, hangar secure."

"Sir. Enemy vessels are picking up speed. Heading in our direction," called the sensor officer.

"All hands, prepare to engage sub-photon drive," called Stellis before nodding to Urutu.

As the ship's main engines roared and the *Cristi* picked up speed, Stellis could see the futile traces of laser fire trailing in its wake.

It was a close call and Stellis was sure Headquarters would not be pleased he was going back without the prize they sent him out to get. That in the end might prove to be of far lesser importance than the fact a Coalition Strike Force was on the scene to contest the retrieval. It was only luck that its commander's eagerness played into the *Cristi*'s hands. That was a slip of major proportions on the part of the enemy but Naval Headquarters couldn't count on having that kind of luck again in the future.

Chapter Four

Murder Trail

Jules sat back in the speedcar as it left the administration dome. He sped toward the northern cluster and dome three. The situation as described by Director Leclerc was concerning enough without his having to tell Joan he'd be leaving in a few days without any definite return date. Adding to the problem was the fact he couldn't explain why he had to leave.

He was still trying to figure a way to broach the subject with her when the speedcar entered the tube connecting with dome three. Taking a drag on an oxygen-tube, he barely felt the 'car come to a halt at the debarking platform beneath the apartment complex where their living unit was housed. He made his way upwards absentmindedly and was about to use his laser key to access Suite 436 when the door opened on its own.

Or rather, Joan opened it.

"I saw you heading up on the monitor," said Joan by way of explanation. "No time for anything else. I got an emergency call from the northwest 'dactor. They said there's a question about the integrity of the nutri-fertilizer content and want me to come and have a look at it. Fly me?"

Somewhat relieved that his news would have to wait, Jules had no problem agreeing to go.

The trip by speedcar back to the rocket field was quickly done and with masks in place, the couple were soon able to access their personal flyer. While Joan went through the safety checks, Jules contacted Control for liftoff instructions.

As it turned out, traffic was light at the moment and they were in the air in no time. Joan ended up doing the flying so Jules sat back and relaxed, watching the green fields of crops surrounding Marsport roll past as the flyer gained altitude.

It was hard to believe that once, before people ever left Earth, there were ethical questions raised about whether man should change anything on Mars or other planetary bodies. *Did they have the right?* those voices wondered.

Jules shook his head. What reason to populate other worlds then? How to maintain colonies and thriving populations? Continue to import everything they needed from Earth and preserve a whole planet as a nature park? The cost/benefit ratio of such an arrangement would have been impossibly out of balance and man's expansion into the cosmos stopped in its tracks. Luckily, however, when men did finally leave the solar system and arrived at other stars, the existence of so many new worlds made the question of planetary conservationism moot. Not that reason didn't prevail even in those early days otherwise there wouldn't have been such an early start terraforming Mars.

"There's the 'dactor," Joan said, snapping Jules from his reverie.

When he looked, he saw they'd passed over a low range of craggy mountains and dropped into the Marinaris Plain where the northwest soil-redactor was hard at work preparing acreage for future tillage. It would be many years before the soil was ready to receive seeds for potatoes, peanuts, or even flowers. First, all the perchlorates, native chemicals that made untreated Martian soil useless for growing any kind of plant life at all, would need to be removed. For that, a special fertilizer prepared from what Jules liked to call anti-perchlorates would need to be introduced. That was the job of giant soil-redactors like the one they were heading out to check on. These monstrous machines, driven from within a control cab, pushed heavy bladed graders extending on a front of hundreds of yards across the tough Martian soil, breaking it up, grinding it down, turning it over, and finally distributing the special fertilizer mix. As it happened, the 'anti-perchlorates' used in the fertilizer mix, was one of Joan's discoveries made on a field trip to Tellus 3 ten years before. It was that discovery that earned her the job with the Geological Survey.

"Why didn't they get one of the engineers to check the fertilizer mix instead of you?" asked Jules as the 'dactor came into sight. "You're not a soil chemist after all."

"Marty wasn't available," Joan explained, looking at something below that caught her eye. "He's off planet attending a conference."

"What's the matter?" questioned Jules, leaning over to try and see what Joan was looking at.

"Don't know. I'm going to swing over and take a closer peek."

So saying, Joan banked the flyer, taking it low over the reddish ground that extended for miles in all directions. It was the featurelessness of the plain that made the object of Joan's attention stand out and easy to spot. As the flyer drew closer, Joan gasped.

"That's a man down there," she said. "He's not moving."

"Set me down and I'll run over and see if he's all right," volunteered Jules. "Once you leave me off, you can get over to the 'dactor and have the operator stop it."

Joan nodded before swinging the flyer about and, expertly hovering a few feet from the dusty ground, let Jules out. With the flyer's dual turbines whining in protest, she pulled away and streaked off in the direction of the soil-redactor.

Jules held his arm up to protect his eyes from the flying dust then ran over to the man lying on the ground. Gently, he turned him over and noticed immediately he wore the coveralls of Interplanetary Reclamations Inc., the contractor that operated the soil-redactors.

The second thing he noticed was the man was dead. Shot through the heart with near surgical precision by a hand-held laser.

Quickly, Jules pulled out his telcomm and called Joan.

In the direction of the soil-redactor, behind the screen of dust that obscured the rows of blades that continued to bite deep into the Martian soil, he could just make out the control cab and the flyer resting on the small heli-pad to its rear.

"Jules, I'm in the cab and nobody's here," came Joan's voice over the telcomm. "The operator's gone."

"He's right here," replied Jules, still eyeing the approaching redactor. "Someone killed him."

"Killed him?"

"Never mind about that for now. Can you stop the 'dactor?" He could hear the operation of the blades clearly now as they dug up the hard surface soil to a depth of three feet and ground the chunks to a fineness conducive to farming. He hated to think what they could do to a human being if one should ever be caught in their path.

"I...I don't know," replied Joan. "I never paid much attention to what the operator was doing the times I came out with Marty. What if I take the flyer out to pick you up?"

"Not enough time," said Jules watching the growing cloud of dust. "Do what you can to stop the 'dactor. I'm going to start running. Maybe I can get out of the way of the blades before they reach me."

Judging the distance to the oncoming redactor, he doubted it but what choice did he have? Putting away his telcomm, he started off, taking a diagonal route that would move him farther away from the approaching redactor while at the same time getting him nearer the end of the long line of blades.

Building up speed, he quickly began to run as fast as he could. His lungs were soon gulping deep drafts of air from an oxygen mask that was not designed for the needs of over exertion. He'd worry about catching his breath afterwards, if he lived. A glance over his shoulder showed that the redactor wasn't stopping. It was getting closer, looming like a juggernaut as its crunching, grinding blades plowed inexorably on. The body of the dead operator disappeared in the dust and noise, leaving no sign at all of having impaired the awful progress of those merciless blades.

Jules tried to pick up speed, but his legs were pumping as fast as he could lift them already. Looking again, he saw the end of the line of blades revealed where a slight breeze brushed away the dust. The weak sun glinted wickedly off the shiny titanium blades that would soon be slicing into his body if he didn't get a move on. Now the redactor was a hundred yards away, now seventy-five, fifty and the sound of the breaking soil and the roar of its twin Cuttner engines filled the whole world. A last desperate look back and Jules thought he saw Joan behind the plas-glass enclosure of the control cab, her fists pounding the 'glass in desperate helplessness. Twenty yards, fifteen, ten! With a last desperate scream of terror, Jules leaped and threw himself outside the perimeter of the final blade, closing his eyes and praying the end would be quick...

The next thing he knew, Joan was holding him, clutching him to her in tearful relief. Rocking him to and fro as he lay on the ground, the sound of the redactor receding into the distance with every second. Suddenly, he clutched her desperately, relieved to still be alive and eager to convince himself of it in the reality of her presence.

"Joan..." was all he could say as he tried to bring the trembling that suddenly overcame him under control.

"Jules, my darling Jules," Joan kept saying. "I thought you were going to die. I thought you were going to die."

"I did too," said Jules, lifting his head. "I don't understand..."

"I was in the control-cab, watching you run. I never felt so helpless in my life. There was nothing I could do. I'd smashed all the instrumentation, but the 'dactor just kept moving. When I couldn't stop it, I ran back to the flyer. It was all I could think of doing. I was horrified when it wouldn't start."

There was a note of rising hysteria in Joan's voice so that Jules tried to calm her down.

"Take it easy," he soothed. "It's all right."

Joan paused, gulping. "I ran back into the cab. I just had to see what was happening with you, but at the last minute, I couldn't take it and hid my eyes. When I dared to look again, I saw you lying off to the side, outside the limit of the blades."

Regaining his nerve, Jules sat up and turned around. He was a good dozen feet from the edge of the newly tilled soil.

"Is this where I fell?" he asked.

"Yes. I jumped from the 'dactor and ran over. This is where I found you."

"How...?" Finally, it dawned on him. Gravity on Mars was only about forty percent that of Earth's. Under normal Terran conditions, he would be dead right now. Because of Mars' lighter gravity, that last leap was enough to have carried him clear of the blades. "How could I have forgotten?"

"What?"

After Jules had explained, they both began to laugh, the relieved, nervous laughter of a close call that could have been the last call for one of them.

Helping each other to their feet, Jules pulled out his telcomm and arranged with the rocket field to send a flyer out to pick them up.

"Jules, what happened to the 'dactor operator?" asked Joan finally. "How did he get out where he was? Who killed him? Why?"

Jules had been wondering about those very things himself and didn't like the answers he was coming up with. Turning to Joan, he filled her in on what he discussed with Director Leclerc and the mission he assigned him to.

"I'm glad you finally came around to telling me," she said when he'd finished.

Jules shrugged. "You didn't give me any time."

"So, do you think this thing with the 'dactor had anything to do with your assignment?" asked Joan. "I mean, how could anyone know I'd get that call from Interplanetary to check their fertilizer mix?"

"They didn't."

"Then how...? Suddenly, it began to dawn on her. "You mean that I...?"

"It's the only answer," said Jules grimly. "They weren't trying to kill me, they were after you."

"Because I knew about you and the incident at Cygnus 12?"

"Right. The body of the operator must have been left on the field like that to lure you into the path of the 'dactor. Naturally, you would've seen there was time to land the flyer to help the man if you could. I'll bet if we checked the flyer right now, we'd find someone fixed it so the engine wouldn't start again after it was shut off."

"I checked the power gauges before we left Marsport," said Joan.

"A gauge needle is mechanical. Easily tampered with."

"It's incredible."

"We need to get you to safety, Joan. No way I'm leaving on that mission knowing you're vulnerable."

"Protective custody? No way. I'll be a virtual prisoner. My work—"

"Can wait if it has to," said Jules grimly. "Honey, this is serious stuff. Whoever tried to kill you isn't going to stop with one failure. They're going to try again. What kind of protection will you have in our suite? At your office or anywhere in between?"

"I won't be any more exposed than you'll be."

"I'll be with a diplomatic team aboard a naval cruiser protected by a tintinabulum shell and a dozen pulse cannons," said Jules with growing impatience. "When we get back, we're going right to Director Leclerc. Do not pass go. Do not collect two hundred dollars."

Joan smiled then and gave in.

"Okay, you win. Now let me contact Marsport Field to get a ride back home."

Feeling exposed standing out in the open the way they were, Jules breathed a sigh of relief when he caught site of the flyer from Marsport streaking in the direction of their signal. In the far distance, a pink smudge on the horizon indicated that the redactor continued on its way, mechanically oblivious to what it had almost done to Jules and what it did do to its former operator, of whom no evidence at all remained, not even a smear of blood.

Jules shivered with the recollection of his near escape and watched as the flyer whined to a rest alongside them. He helped Joan inside before following her aboard, and soon they were being whisked by automatic pilot back to Marsport.

Amid the bustling throngs of the city, Jules' spirits lifted so he could concentrate on Joan's safety. Wondering if they should stop at their suite first before heading to the administrative dome and Military Intelligence, he decided to take no chances.

"Joan, I want us to go directly to dome one. We can't take a chance that while we were gone, some other trap has been prepared at our suite to catch me."

"You really think there might be danger there? If it weren't for what we've just been through, I'd suspect you of being paranoid."

Jules took a long drag on an oxygen tube to give him time to think. Around them, the main concourse of dome seven, in the lengthening shadow of the crater rim where Marsport Field was located, thousands of residents came and went oblivious to the hidden dangers that threatened he and Joan.

Steering Joan toward an approaching speedcar, Jules' signaled for a halt and they climbed in.

"Dome one," said Jules as the speedcar beeped and booped in response and exited the siding. In seconds, it merged with other 'cars, switched lanes and headed down the tube that connected with dome six and beyond.

"It's not paranoia, Joan," said Jules finally. "This game is very real. What we discovered on Cygnus 12 is radical, dangerous technology and for whichever side in the war that can master it, it means victory. I don't have to tell you what that would be like if that victor is the Coalition. Right now, the enemy is losing this war and that makes them more dangerous than ever. If they feel themselves being backed into a corner, they'll get desperate. They've already killed hundreds of thousands of people in the war, and it's not likely they're going to stop at two more. Our lives mean nothing to them. The black hole tech we discovered does, and they'll not stop at nothing to keep us from learning the secret of its containment. That's what makes us so dangerous to their plans. They know that somehow we managed to get that artificial black hole under control. With that knowledge, they have no other choice but to believe the Consortium will move full speed ahead to develop the technology and put a quick end to the war. An end not in the Coalition's favor."

Joan was silent when Jules finished and only stared ahead into the single lane tube that connected dome two to dome one.

Hoping he'd finally convinced his wife of the very real danger that threatened them, Jules allowed himself to relax as the speedcar slid into the MI's dedicated entry area.

Chapter Five

Summit Meeting

Looking around the room, Jules missed his wife.

It was two weeks later. Two weeks spent mostly cooped up in a cramped Naval ship as it transited millions of parsecs of space via sub-photon drive that left everyone aboard exhausted. Now, they had reached their destination, one that Jules only learned after Task Force 8 abandoned thrusters for sub-photon drive out past the orbit of Pluto.

It was an ice world of perpetual winter. It had no name only a number, one Jules promptly had forgotten. He only knew it was in the constellation Piscus Autrinus located far enough from either the Consortium or Coalition territory that neither was interested in it. As good a place as any for a meeting on neutral ground.

Right now, he was in the day room of the *St. Peter*, Admiral Freeman's flag ship. Not that day room meant it was very big. No single space within a Naval ship could be considered roomy. That was why it seemed so crowded at the moment. There was the Exterior Minister himself, Alistair Jones, his first assistant Bentley O'Shea, and the secretary they shared, Manda Mooney. Jules took a moment to admire Miss Mooney. A very attractive woman, and one who hadn't been shy about flirting with him during the voyage, even with his wedding band prominently featured on his finger. Generally speaking, the Consortium frowned on single women traveling on government vessels, but sometimes exceptions had to be made.

It was a rule Jules could live with, except this time he was traveling on his own. After the two attempts on their lives back on Mars, there was no question about placing Joan into protective custody. After the attempt on their lives back on Mars...

Naturally, she didn't like the idea but common sense prevailed. Director Leclerc provided her with a suite in dome one where security was tighter as a matter of course, and Joan would have a pair of bodyguards with her at all times whenever she left it.

Her safety became even more imperative after she and Jules arrived at Military Intelligence only to discover that there'd been a battle at Cygnus 12. Coalition vessels appeared in the system just at the moment when the Navy was about to recover the enemy wreck. No way that could have happened by accident. The Coalition knew about the recovery operation, leaving no other conclusion than the elements of his report to MI had been leaked. After that, his role with the current diplomatic mission became even more important.

Until the leak was identified, Jules was aware his life was in constant danger. Anyone aboard the *St. Peter* could be an enemy agent, and looking around the crowded room, he surveyed the possibilities.

Talking with Admiral Freeman were a number of his officers as well as the military liaison Col. Ivor Swenson. Both had been notified of the danger but were doing a good job at hiding their concerns, if they had any.

The rest of the crowd consisted of various scientific advisers, cultural historians versed in everything from Coalition military strategy to social customs, and the all-important translators.

Not for the first time, Jules wished there were some view ports in the room so he'd have some place to look without the danger of making eye contact with someone, but it was not to be. Dr. Marta Sandoz spotted him as his gaze swept past her. She decided to come over and keep him company.

"You look a little lost," said Sandoz, one of the delegation's science advisers. As a psycho-xenologist, she specialized in how aliens did their thinking. A valuable skill in any negotiations like the ones due to begin in a few hours.

"Do I?"

"If I don't miss my guess, you're not especially happy to be here."

"Is that your diagnosis, doctor?"

"No, it's what anyone could tell just by looking at you."

"Well, you're right, however you figured it. I'd just gotten back from a deep space survey when I was drafted for this mission. I was looking forward to some down time...with my wife."

"That explains it, I guess," said Sandoz, sipping at a vacuum drink.

"So, I hear you've done this sort of thing before. Do you expect to be able to tell what the Coalition representatives will be thinking?"

"Not what they're thinking," corrected Sandoz. "A psycho-xenologist can only study behavior and extrapolate thought *patterns*, there's a big difference."

"What difference exactly?" asked Jules, genuinely interested.

"Well, I don't read minds for instance." she laughed as though she'd made a joke no one else understood. "Depending on specialty, and mine concentrated on the three major Coalition races, the Drool, Sangi, and Zhapoologani, psycho-xenologists study all they can about non-Terran races, culture, military, religion. We especially concentrate on their cultural myths and legends to identify the root inspirations for societal behavior. Once we've mastered that, we can predict present day thought patterns with a fair degree of accuracy."

"Just what will you be looking for during the negotiations?"

"That depends on what the negotiators bring to the table and what race they are. There are a couple of my colleagues here who specialize in some of the Coalition's junior partners just in case, but it's not likely the Drool, for instance, will allow that."

"Why not?"

"The Coalition practices what might be called a caste system that's pretty rigid. It's not exactly comparable to those systems we've had on Earth, but something like it. No way a junior partner like the Joviani would ever be invited to an important meeting like this."

"Does that make the job easier?"

"For me it does," Sandoz laughed again.

She did that easily. Jules was finding that if it were not for Joan, he'd be mightily attracted to the dark-haired psycho-xenologist.

"Will you tell me?" asked Jules. "Knowing what you do of how the Coalition thinks, will having to leave behind one of the ships in the task force make any difference?"

"You mean if having only four ships along instead of five will make a difference in intimidating them? No. One ship won't make a difference. After half a century of warfare with the Consortium and losing ground so I'm told, they know enough by now not to underestimate us. In fact, if it weren't for this black hole thing, my guess is that they'd be coming to the bargaining table to talk peace not war."

"You think so?"

"Yes, I do."

Before Jules could press her further on her belief, a high-pitched whistle came over the intercom, and the admiral announced that the Coalition Strike Group had arrived.

"Oh, good," said Sandoz. "They won't want to waste any time now and get started."

"Is that SOP?"

"For the Coalition it is."

"They won't even send a team down to the planet's surface to review our preparations?"

"It's part of their cultural protocol. When meeting someone, it's expected that the first to arrive will have everything prepared and proper. We've done that."

"On your advice?"

"Yes and no. I'm part of a team after all."

With that, everyone in the room whose presence was expected at the negotiations was asked to report to the ship's hangar to catch transport planetside. Jules joined the science advisers and soon found himself strapped in to a shuttle ready to go. Launch was made without any special ceremony and the next thing he knew, they had joined a small flotilla of surface to air craft that escorted them through the wispy atmosphere. Jules could barely see a thing through the small porthole near his seat, but what he saw was enough to confirm that the planet was covered in ice and snow and as it all rushed up to meet them, all detail was lost in the blinding whiteness.

The trip down was really quite comfortable, and the shuttle's insulation such that no sound of rushing wind could be heard in the cabin. Jules found himself looking for Sandoz and spotted her sitting with the translators. She, at least, seemed to be taking the descent in stride. He hardly had time to think any further before he felt the thrusters cut off and the whine of the air foils kick in for the final approach. He couldn't see it, but he imagined the temporary signal lights flashing, allowing the pilots visual direction the last few hundred feet down. His thoughts were confirmed when he felt the gentle bump of a soft landing and the cabin lights brighten, indicating touchdown.

As with civilians anywhere, his fellow passengers hardly waited until the shuttle was secure before leaping from their seats and crowding toward the exit. When Jules finally made it himself, he stepped into an embarkation tunnel of toughened plastic that led about one hundred feet to a membrane giving access to the main portion of the all-weather temp-structure. It was designed to be set up quickly in any kind of hostile environment so long as there was an atmosphere. He knew from earlier briefings that the embarkation tunnel had its duplicate on the opposite side for use by the Coalition delegation.

"Exciting, isn't it?"

Jules turned to see Mooney using the press of bodies to get close to him.

"Hope it all doesn't turn out to be anti-climactic," said Jules.

"Oh, I don't think so. It's not every day we get to see a Zhapoologani up close."

"You never saw one before?"

"Only on the 'casts. You?"

"I've seen some action once or twice. Bumped into some of their troopers."

"Really? That's interesting. You'll have to tell me more about it on the flight back."

Jules decided to change the subject, hoping she'd forget about any lengthy talk. "Any idea how your boss intends to approach the Zhapoologani? They're not exactly what you'd call loquacious fellows."

"Oh, Minister Jones is quite savvy. He knows how to get people to talk..."

"People, maybe."

"An unbeliever, are we? You'll see...oh, Bentley wants me."

Walking back from the head of the line, O'Shea reached them giving, Jules only a perfunctory nod.

"Manda, Minister Jones wants to see you. Wants to make sure he's got the protocol down."

"Right," responded Mooney. "I'll talk to you later, Jules."

Jules looked after her a moment, admiring her figure. Well, Joan always told him that it was all right to look so long as he didn't touch...

Moving along, he noticed that there were no armed guards in sight. That came as no surprise to Jules as he had been briefed on protocol. The two sides had done this kind of thing often enough over the years that a level of trust had been established. Besides, they each had reason to keep the lines of communication open.

Stepping through the membrane, Jules followed directions given by O'Shea as he arranged everyone according to pre-set plans. Sandoz joined the translators at a table inlaid with computer screens and speakers. There, she sat down, inserting an earpiece discreetly under her hair.

Exterior Minister Alistair Jones took a seat at another table located in the center of the room; a plastoid curtain hung rigidly in front of him hiding activity on the other side which Jules could make out only as vague movements

After directing the science contingent to stand at the back of the room, O'Shea took his place on Jones' right while Mooney took hers on the left. Someone must have signaled that everything was ready because without any notice, the curtain in front of the negotiating team parted revealing a similar arrangement on the other side.

It was the Zhapoologani all right. Jules glanced at Sandoz who was suddenly the center of attention among the translators who instantly began whispering together, no doubt comparing notes on what they knew about the Coalition representatives.

The Zhapoologani delegate, from what Jules could see, differed little in appearance from the few Coalition troopers of his race that he had seen before. Human-like in general outline except for being a good deal huskier in the torso, his arms were thinner than those of human beings while his legs thicker. A bullet head hunched heavily on his broad shoulders that showed little neck. Rough, tannish skin or hide covered the hairless body as tiny eyes squinted out at the Terran contingent seated across the table. Like others of his kind, the Zhapoologani wore little in the way of clothes except for an embroidered breech cloth of some kind and heraldic ensigns displayed on a colorful sash that banded the chest. There was one other Zhapoologani standing behind him, the rest of the contingent seemed to be Drools whose gray skin looked oily in the room's light. Their heads were featureless, lacking in sensory organs of any kind while the rest of their bodies lay hidden in thick folds of lunnite cloth, a material intended to protect them from ambient germs present in the cleanest of atmospheres.

Jules knew it wasn't right, but he couldn't help feeling uncomfortable in their presence, something he knew was based solely on their physical appearance. He could never decide if it was a natural human reaction to the unearthly or a personal prejudice that he needed to overcome.

He had no time to think on the issue further as the opening pleasantries were concluded and Jones signaled for him to approach the table.

"Dr. Santros is one our top physicists who was involved in research dealing with black hole technology," Jones was saying to the Zhapoologani ambassador. "He will now explain the situation that prompted us to call this meeting."

O'Shea stood and waved Jules over to the table, holding out is arm to stop him well short of where he and Jones sat. When O'Shea retook his seat, Jones nodded and Jules, in well-rehearsed words, began to recount his experience on Cygnus Alpha 12. When he finished, he let the translator catch up before concluding with a few remarks about the danger for everyone should black hole technology be used, especially in warships.

Throughout his summation, he could not tell from the expression on the Zhapoologani's face what the creature was thinking. He prayed that his words had been chosen correctly to adequately convey the seriousness of the subject.

"So you see, ambassador Keestofernomi," Jones said, "just as we already have agreed on a ban covering atomics, we believe this new technology may be even more dangerous, threatening the entire galaxy rather than single worlds. Black hole technology presents the possibility of even more uncontrollable consequences should its natural energies be released. As yet, neither of our two sides have developed reliable methods for its containment, and from what our scientists say, nor are likely ever to do so."

"We are not unmindful of the danger," rumbled the Zhapoologani.

"Then the Coalition is open to an agreement?"

"Perhaps," said the Zhapoologani carefully. "What assurances do we have...?

"I think the Consortium's history in adhering to our agreements regarding the use of atomics speaks for itself while our unilateral choice not to use germ, DNA, or other weapons of indiscriminate death speaks to our good intentions."

"Sometimes good intentions can be self-serving, can they not?"

"They can," admitted Jones. "Regardless of the intention, the actions are real."

"You do not want to despoil worlds that you may later wish to colonize."

"True again, but there is no guarantee victory will be the Consortium's in our contest."

"I am glad to hear you Terrans are not so overconfident you minimize the power of the Outer Arm Coalition," said the Zhapoologani with a hint of pride.

"The Consortium takes nothing for granted," said Jones, diplomatically.

At that point, the Zhapoologani leaned over to the Drool sitting beside him and the two held a brief conference, the gist of which could not be heard by the translators. Finished, the ambassador signaled for someone in the delegation behind him, and another of his race thumped over to join those at the table. More low-key words as Jules guessed the newcomer was likely his counterpart in the Coalition's delegation.

Finished, the Zhapoologani turned back to Jones and began to speak.

"Exterior Minister Jones, the Outer Arm Coalition is prepared to —"

Just then, there was a late arrival on the Coalition side of the room who called something out that stopped the Zhapoologani in mid-sentence. From his body language, Jules could tell the ambassador was annoyed. He turned abruptly to face the cause of the disturbance and after a moment, another Drool, after apparently receiving the message brought by the newcomer, approached the ambassador and whispered in the orifice in the side of his head that passed for an ear. Instantly, the Zhapoologani became alert and turning back to Jones, angrily berated him!

"So, you believed you could treat us like fools," he thundered, rising to his feet. "This has been a direct insult to the honor of the Coalition. Think you that we would not discover your perfidy? Pfah, on your negotiations."

By that time, Jones' face had turned a beet red and he too shot to his feet, quickly followed by O'Shea.

"What is the meaning of this about face, Keestofernomi?" he asked. "By what right do you make such an accusation?"

"By what right? By right of betrayal. By right of violation of diplomatic trust."

"In what way have we violated diplomatic trust? You must offer proof."

"Proof is it? I will give you proof. The Coalition is not without its resources, and those resources tell us that one of your own naval ships has been reserved and sent on a secret mission to develop the very black hole technology that you have been at this table trying to convince the Coalition to leave aside!"

"What ship? I have no knowledge of this."

"Furthermore, this information casts a different light on your doings at Cygnus 12."

"Cygnus 12?" Jones seemed genuinely surprised, and Jules wondered if he'd been informed about that mission.

"Oh, you are very good, Exterior Minister Jones. You lie well. Fortunately, our sources are quite as good and they do not lie. There will be no agreement this day, Exterior Minister Jones."

By that point, people on both sides of the room were talking with voices being raised on all sides. Meaningful communications broke down, and the meeting ended in much mutual acrimony and accusation. The bottom line was that not only would there be no deal, but the Coalition vowed to continue its research into black hole technology, the very thing the Terrans hoped the summit would help to avoid.

Chapter Six

Cabal

The next few days were dominated by angry recriminations with the diplomatic team blaming military intelligence for not keeping them informed and scientists wringing their hands warning something must be done to salvage the negotiations. What it all ended up being was a lot of heat but no light. When the two-week journey back to Sol was over, not much more was learned than what was known in those first few days.

For his part, Jules felt as if the trip lasted six months instead of just one. Time stretched out endlessly as he waited to get back to Mars and Director Leclerc to find out what the real lowdown was.

Now he was looking out at the same view of farmland and distant desert but somehow, it wasn't the same as it appeared the last time he saw it. It didn't *look* different, but his perception of it had changed. With the black hole tech genie out of its bottle, there was a good chance all of it might just disappear as if it never existed. Everything, he realized, all reality, had become ephemeral, uncertain, impermanent...

"...have to do something about this and fast," Leclerc was saying from behind his workstation.

His words jarred Jules from his reverie as he turned his attention back to the meeting at hand. Frustrated that he'd not been able to see Joan before finding himself in the director's office again, he'd been summoned there by Leclerc for he knew not what. In fact, he doubted that anyone, including the director, really knew what came next.

"So, what happened?" asked Jules by way of breaking the tension and getting whatever conversation Leclerc had in mind started. "Were they telling us the truth? Were we just used as pawns to get the Coalition to stop its research to give our side time to get it first?"

"Absolutely not," insisted Leclerc.

"Why didn't our side know about that ship?"

"Because the Navy didn't get word to us in time," said Leclerc. "They were more worried about covering their backsides than anything else. The *John Crosse* was left behind when a crack was supposedly found in its thruster housing. As things turned out, that wasn't the case because a few days after the Task Force left the system, it disappeared. The Navy wasted over a week trying to find out what happened to it before finally having to admit that one of their ships went missing."

"Sabotage then?"

"Maybe, or someone just made it look that way. We're leaning on that explanation because the ship was obviously stolen, it didn't just disappear. Checking back, the best our people can figure, the ship's computers were hacked and shipyard workers given a false reading about the housings. That was enough to keep the ship from joining the Task Force and would have reduced the crew to a minimum while the housing awaited repair. From there, who knows what happened. Maybe the remaining crew were in on the theft or were just taken along with the ship. Where it is now is anyone's guess.

"As to the Coalition delegation, the only way they could have known about the theft before we did is by having an informant inside the Naval Office."

"It's possible the thieves told them," said Jules.

"What makes you say that?"

"To throw us off balance?" Jules offered. "It might be they wanted to force the Consortium to take up the black hole research again? After all, if the Coalition is going at it, we can't just stand by and let it happen. In any case, we've likely got an arms race on our hands."

"Unless we find that ship," said Leclerc. "If we can bring the thieves in soon enough and prove the Consortium wasn't trying to double cross the Coalition, there might still be a chance to stop that arms race before it begins."

"Okay, but where do you start?"

"Well, we haven't been idle while you were making your way back from Piscus Autrinus," said Leclerc. "Our boys figure the reason why the

John Crosse was taken was because it was a deep range ship. Only Naval ships. as you know, have the capability of inter-stellar travel...except for the big liners, there aren't any commercial models that can do that. So, wherever the thieves were going, it was likely out of the solar system."

"That's logical...unless it's a ruse. They took a deep range vessel with the intention of making you look for them in the wrong place."

"We thought of that, which means we're going to look everywhere for them. No stone left unturned and all that. I personally doubt they're still in the solar system. Too hard to hide a Navy ship for long, and the operation was far too chancy to be just a ruse."

"All right. Assuming they're no longer in the solar system, where would they go? What's the range of the *John Crosse*?"

"You know that," rejoined Leclerc. "Virtually unlimited. The only restrictive factor would be time. How much of it would they need to get wherever it is they were going?"

"Well. it sounds like you've hit a wall with this," said Jules, pausing to take a drag on his 'tube. "With the whole galaxy to hide in you'll never find them."

"That's where you come in, Jules."

"Me? How can I help?"

Leclerc stood and came around his workstation. "When they hacked the ship's computers, they left their fingerprints, so to speak. Not to get into too much detail, but some years ago the military's cyber-warfare division was able to develop a program that could trace back any attempt to break into our computer systems."

"Are you saying they were able to identify who the thieves were?" asked Jules, leaning forward in his chair. "Well, who are they?"

"Take it easy. You're not going to like this. The signals were traced back to our own labs downstairs..."

"The Science Division?"

"More specifically, your old black hole tech research group."

Jules sat stunned, his 'tube hanging limply between his fingers.

"We checked the records and found that a few of our top men put in for leaves of absence just before the *John Crosse* disappeared," the director was saying. "Including Ivar Stolius, our cyber specialist. He had just the know how that could make the theft of the Navy ship possible."

"I don't believe it," declared Jules. "Our people are too dedicated to...besides, they were all vetted and back checked every which way from..."

The director was shaking his head.

"I'll be honest, we found nothing. These guys, Stolius, Henry Martine, and a few others didn't do this for the usual reasons that treason is committed. They did it for other purposes."

"What purposes?"

"That's what I want you to find out...after you track them down."

"Me? What makes you think I can do any better than the whole service..."

"Because you knew these guys. You worked side by side with them for years. You must have figured out how they think...what they think. There must be some clue in some past conversation you had with them that could lead you to them. Frankly, we've got nothing else to go on. We have men watching their homes, their family members, tapping their holo-phones, their home and office workstations in case they try to access them remotely. We've come up with nothing so far."

"So, what more do you think I—"

"I don't know, Jules," shouted Leclerc, losing his patience. "Think of something. Talk to their friends, their wives, kids...anything but get us something to work on."

Jules waited a few seconds to let things calm down. After a moment of contemplation, he asked, "Do you have the rest of those names for me?"

Chapter Seven

Flashpoint

The *Golgotha* and its escorts rode in orbit well away from the corona of the main sequence star Betelgeuse in the constellation Orion but still within its gravitational flux. Remaining within the shadow of the flux was important in order to keep the task force hidden from Coalition deep range scanners.

At six hundred and forty light years from Sol, Betelgeuse was among the star systems under dispute between the Terran Consortium and the Outer Arm Coalition whose nearest settlements were well within sensor range of the *Golgotha.* Accompanied by a trio of sleek destroyers and an equal number of cruisers, the Terran battleship's signal was boosted by the combined power generated by her six escorts

It was vital that the task force remain undiscovered as Admiral Dalton Blaine had orders to simply eavesdrop on Coalition communications and track local stellar traffic. He was to avoid battle. It rankled Blaine somewhat not to be able to initiate action if it was necessary, but hardcopy orders opened only once the task force was underway revealed some Coalition ships could be equipped with dangerous black hole tech and until the Consortium could find a way to neutralize it or talk the Coalition into abandoning it, risk of rupturing the tech's containment housing could not be hazarded. Thus, in case of a confrontation, Blaine had orders to defend himself but also to break off and retreat at the first opportunity.

Those orders were about to be put to the test when a disturbance in the star's magnetic flux drew the attention of the watch officer.

"Sir," he called out. "I have enemy cruisers off our port bow."

"What? Why weren't they detected before now?" demanded a

suddenly alert Blaine.

"Sir. They weren't there a moment ago...they just...are there now."

"They must be using that damned black hole tech, sir," said the XO.

"Must be. Helm, evasive action, Sparks, notify the rest of the task force to do the same and reassemble at point epsilon."

"Yes, sir," came the simultaneous replies.

"Mr. Silko," said Blaine, turning to his XO. "Take over fire control. Targeted lasers only. No pulse cannons."

"Yes, sir." Saluting, the XO dashed to the weapons console to direct fire personally. It was vital that the men not let their eagerness for battle get the best of them. The targeted lasers were light weapons used largely to disable.

"Target enemy thruster housings only," reminded Blaine. "Avoid damaging the engine sections where the tech is likely to be stored."

"Yes, sir," called back Silko.

Outside, in the super-hot glare of the giant sun, the *Golgotha* had already begun to come about, bringing its port gun emplacements to bear toward the Coalition battlewagon that had so suddenly come out of nowhere to take the first shot.

BLANG!

Struck while the *Golgotha* was in mid turn, the blow of the Coalition ion borer missed hitting full broadside, deflecting most of its energy off the Terran vessel's tintinabulum hull.

"One shot is all they get," growled one of the weaponeers from fire control before letting loose a laser blast of his own.

With its full port side now facing the enemy ship, the *Golgotha* was able to fire all of its guns at once, the force of which cut the Coalition ship's thruster housings point blank. Instantly, its propulsive power was diminished to nothing, rendering the huge vessel dead in space.

There was a howl of glee from a number of the ship's crew and even Blaine allowed himself a bit of a smile before recalling that they had been taken completely by surprise in the sneak attack. How had the enemy known the Terrans would be here? The admiral recalled how the Coalition delegation in recent negotiations learned of the stolen *John Crosse* before its Terran counterparts did. That time, it was determined spies back in the

Sol system had been the informants. Could that have happened again here? How else would the Coalition have learned of the task force's presence?

BLANG! BLANG!

The sounds of the hits and the resultant shudder that coursed through the ship jolted Blaine's thoughts back to the present.

"Damn it, where are our escorts? Why aren't they drawing fire?"

"Sir," cried the XO, "the *Red Sea* and the *Halo* are damaged, the *Santo Dominguez* is exchanging fire with two enemy K-class cruisers, and the *Jerusalem, San Antonio*, and *Ste. Marguerite* are chasing off a pair of light cruisers."

"So, what hit us?"

"There was another heavy battlewagon positioned behind the first one we disabled, sir."

"Helm, hard about and down forty degrees. We'll take that ship in the belly."

"Yes, sir."

Even as he spoke, Blaine felt the *Golgotha* sink beneath him as the artificial gravity strained at the shift in angle. On the bow screens, he saw the disabled battlewagon up ahead with its mangled thruster housings sparking away as it slid upward and disappeared from view. Suddenly, the second Coalition battlewagon loomed up ahead.

"Bow lasers, prepare to fire," he called.

"Bow lasers are green, sir,"

"Target thruster housings."

"Thruster housings targeted, sir."

"Fire."

For a moment, the glare of the lasers filled the screen, blinding Blaine. When it cleared, the enemy ship showed damage to its thrusters, but there was no time to congratulate themselves as the watch officer called out again.

"Sir. More enemy ships have arrived."

"Sparks," said Blaine, recalling his orders, "have all ships turn about and assemble at point epsilon."

"Point epsilon, yes, sir."

It was touch and go for a while with the *Golgotha* having to train its lasers once more on enemy vessels to take pressure off the *Santo Dominguez* while the *Red Sea* and the *Halo* were taken into tow with tractor beams. Finally, they all managed to assemble at point epsilon. Though it rankled Blaine to do it, he gave the order to fire up the sub-photon drive engines and retreat. Luckily, it seemed, ships moving alo ng with sub-photon drive presented too fast a target for black hole tech to be used to its best advantage. Still, retreat was retreat, and unless something was not done to neutralize the enemy's technical advantage, Blaine feared the days of the Consortium being a major power in the galaxy were numbered.

Chapter Eight

Death Run

"I feel like I've been given a limited parole," whispered Joan as she and Jules made their entrance to the diplomatic banquet held to bid Exterior Minister Alistair Jones farewell as he prepared to leave for Earth the next day.

Jules patted her hand where it rested in the crook of his arm. "Take it easy."

"Hmph."

"Remember, we're here on business."

"Hmph," grunted Joan again. "Some business. I'm just window dressing."

"Not at all," assured Jules, scanning the crowd of dignitaries, military officials, Marsport administrators, and hangers on. "Your protective coloration. People will talk to us more freely if they see that we're just an ordinary couple enjoying a pleasant evening out."

"I wish we were."

"Time to get to work, so put on your most disarming smile."

Joan used her fingers to push up the corners of her mouth. "How's this?"

Jules rolled his eyes and Joan laughed, for real this time.

"Dr. Santros." A portly man of middle age approached them with a small glass in his hand. "And this must be the charming Mrs. Santros our soil reclamation people have spoken to me about."

"Mr. Belldur," returned Jules. "Joan, I'd like you to meet the chief administrator of Marsport."

"A pleasure," said Joan, all smiles.

"Let me apologize again for that incident with the runaway

44

'dactor," Belldur was saying. "Something like that has never happened before. Completely without precedent. You can't imagine how relieved we all were to learn neither you nor your husband was killed."

"It's only too bad the same couldn't be said for the operator," said Joan with a straight face.

"That was unfortunate, of course."

"Has anything been turned up by the investigation, Mr. Belldur?" asked Jules.

"Nothing that I've heard. Maybe Mr. Tenbro knows more." He looked around quickly before spotting the Interplanetary Reclamation Inc. representative on the other side of the room. Catching his eye, he signaled for him to come over.

When the contractor drew up, Belldur made introductions all around.

"Call me Will," said Tenbro, who had a face that looked like it had been weathered in the climes of a half dozen worlds.

"Jules here was just asking if any progress had been made in finding out who killed the operator of the northwest 'dactor," said Belldur.

Tenbro sipped his drink before replying. "I'm afraid we haven't made much progress. As you know, the operator's body was completely destroyed when the 'dactor passed over him. Likewise, for any telltale markings on the ground that might have suggested how he got there. No DNA residue left in the cab as well, except for those of the operator. The police even scanned cab surfaces for finger prints but found nothing. Witnesses in the hills, a few wildcat miners, said they saw two flyers head out to the 'dactor, one about ten minutes before the other. That suggests someone knew you were on your way and was ready to act as soon as they got word. Because of the speed of the 'dactor, the timing had to be precise."

"These people knew what they were doing. Could they have been employees of the company?" asked Jules, thinking that Tenbro himself would have been in the perfect position to coordinate such a plan.

"We've combed through our records and found nothing in the backgrounds of any of our employees that would suggest a criminal history," replied Tenbro.

"What about the operator's log?" wondered Jules. "The cab's

computer must have registered any flyer that used the heli-pad."

Tenbro shrugged. "Unfortunately, the computer log was erased. Whoever the killer was, they knew enough to bring along an electromagnetic scrambler. Besides erasing the computer log, it also destroyed the 'dactor's programming, explaining why it didn't stop as soon as your wife began tampering with the control systems."

"I assure you, Dr. Santros, that the Police Department will remain on this case until the culprits are found," said Belldur. "Marsport is known as a peaceful community and doesn't need this kind of activity to tarnish its reputation."

"I appreciate that, Mr. Belldur," said Jules.

"Honey, I think I see someone over here who wants to talk with you," said Joan, tugging at his arm.

It was Bentley O'Shea, neat in a dark, collarless tux.

"Sorry to interrupt, but the minister was wondering if he could have a few words with Dr. Santros before he leaves," said O'Shea.

"By all means," replied Belldur.

"Gentlemen," said Jules, allowing Joan to lead him away.

Skirting the dance floor where a number of couples were moving to the strains of the latest swing-jazz fusion, Jules followed O'Shea to the opposite side of the room. There, bodyguards trying to look like ordinary guests maintained a clear space around Exterior Minister Alistair Jones, Colonel Ivor Swenson, and Admiral Jon Freeman.

"Ah, Dr. Santros," greeted Jones, extending a hand.

"Minister Jones," said Jules. "My wife, Mrs. Santros."

"Charmed. Of course you know Admiral Freeman and Colonel Swenson?"

Jules said yes realizing that the introductions were directed mostly at Joan.

Lowering his voice slightly, Jones continued. "Has there been any more word about the *John Crosse*, Dr. Santros?"

"Why do you ask me?" asked Jules, instantly wary.

"We've been briefed by Military Intelligence on efforts being made to trace the *John Crosse*," explained Freeman. "The Navy, of course, is interested in the matter."

To say the least, thought Jules. "Your briefing included mention of myself...?"

"Director Leclerc did say he had assigned you to the investigative team," noted Jones.

"Well, in that case, no, there has been no new information about the case," said Jules guardedly. "I haven't been called off, so I intend to proceed with my end of the investigation."

"Which is?" asked Swenson.

Jules was quite aware that security had been Swenson's responsibility during the diplomatic mission to Piscus Autrinus when somehow, word had been given to the Coalition delegation about the missing *John Crosse.*

"Right now," said Jules carefully, "I'm questioning some of my former colleagues in the Science Division, a couple of whom are attending this function, I understand."

"You were with the Science Division?" asked Freeman. "I understood that you were employed by the Interplanetary Geological Survey."

"I was, still am, actually," replied Jules. "I was asked in on the Coalition negotiations by MI on the basis of my experience with black hole technology. My services have since been requested for part of the ongoing investigation."

"Any progress in that regard?" asked the minister.

"I'm afraid not. The whereabouts of some of my former colleagues with whom MI would most like to speak are still unknown, and family members and or acquaintances who remain on Mars have expressed ignorance as to where they might have gone."

"Very delicately put, doctor," said Swenson. "I assume those people are being monitored just the same?"

"In fact, they've been placed in protective custody," replied Jules, sensing Joan's hand stiffen on his arm.

"The *John Crosse* must be found," said Freeman urgently. "It's just intolerable that a warship in the Consortium Navy could simply be stolen by parties unknown."

"If it's any consolation, admiral, whoever took it were no ordinary hijackers or thieves," soothed Jules. "This was a very well-conceived operation conducted by some of the most brilliant minds in the Consortium. They wouldn't have been working for the Science Division if they weren't."

"That's cold comfort, doctor, with careers on the line," grumbled Freeman.

Jules judged it more diplomatic to say nothing.

"Then you won't mind if I move on with my duties, gentlemen," Jules said, "I think I see a couple of those former colleagues I mentioned."

"Well, I was pretty much frozen out of that conversation," said Joan once they were out of earshot.

"There was definitely some tension there. Enough to cut it with a knife."

"You think? Freeman was getting a little testy."

"I'd be worried about my braids, too, if I were an admiral with a stolen battlewagon."

"I think the admiral doth protest too much."

Jules laughed. "Now I know why I brought you. You're a human lie detector."

"Well, look who crashed the party," called Henry Clyde from where he stood with Sau Kadaka sampling some Martian beer.

"Henry, Sau," acknowledged Jules. "You guys know Joan..."

"Prettier than ever," said Kadaka.

"Thank you, kind sir," said Joan, sketching a curtsey.

"If I didn't get that transfer to Io, it'd be me on her arm instead of you Jules," said Henry good naturedly.

"Weren't you married at the time, Henry?" teased Joan.

"Didn't matter," said Henry.

"I think that beer has gone to your head, Henry," said Jules, smiling. "The grain and hops growth factors still need some work."

"Nonsense, tastes great," said Henry, taking another swallow.

"Director Leclerc has put you on the trail of a number of the Science Division's employees I hear," said Kadaka, by way of getting down to business.

"Right." Jules looked around and lowered his voice. "You know what the situation is. A number of the boys in Science Division applied for and got leaves of absence. I'm trying to track them down. Because neither of you have applied for leaves, you've largely been cleared in regards to the theft of the *John Crosse*. Besides, Henry has been out of the picture on Io for some time and you've been Division Super right along. I won't insult your intelligence by suggesting you haven't been checked out every way there is. You have and you've been found clean."

Kadaka nodded.

"It was still your signature on those leaves," pointed out Jules.

"We were between projects," explained Kadaka. "There was some downtime. It's been the practice of the department when that happens to grant leaves to employees who want to visit family or give some attention to neglected business at home. I saw nothing wrong with that."

"What about those who applied for leaves, did any of their reasons strike you as unusual?"

Kadaka shrugged. "Nothing unexpected."

"Did any of them ask to go off planet?"

"Not that I know of. They all live hereabouts in Marsport anyway except Davis, his family is out Redrock Dome way. His wife is an advisor for the Native Species Development Commission there if you'll recall."

"Can you forward to my telcomm all of their addresses? I'll need to check them out."

"No problem."

"Anybody else I should be looking into? Anybody who may not have filed for a leave but has still been out of the picture?"

Kadaka thought a moment before supplying a name. "Georg Heintzle. You remember him?"

"Of course. But only on a professional level. He specialized in quantum mechanics, didn't he?"

"Right. His latest research on transferring information along open timeline curves on a quantum level could speed communications to the nth degree without the predicted causality issues."

"Now I remember. He isn't with the Science Division at the moment?"

"He quit the Division a few months ago, well ahead of the recent leave requests. Do you think that's suspicious?"

"Don't know. Right now, I can't afford to ignore anything. Thanks, Sau. Don't forget to shoot me that other information, okay?"

"I'll do it right now," said Kadaka, pulling out his own telcomm.

"Will you gentlemen excuse me?" asked Joan. "I'm just going to grab myself a drink."

"Guess that's my cue to leave too," said Jules. "Oh, and I'd appreciate it if you guys keep mum about my investigation."

Quickly, Jules caught up with his wife, touching her elbow as she made her way to the bar. The affair was in full swing by this time with the dance floor crowded and guests laughing and talking in raised voices to be heard over the hubbub.

Taking a pinch of her crinosynth gown between her fingers, Joan climbed the few steps up to the banquet hall's main platform where guests were clustered around self-heating tables displaying an array of hors d'oeuvres popular in six systems.

"The watering hole's this way, I think," said Jules, nodding his head in the direction of the bar.

"I'm like a horse, I can smell water," replied Joan, heading to the sound of tinkling glasses.

As they drew near the bar, Jules caught a familiar sight. Standing apart from the crowd was a woman in green crinosynth, her black hair piled atop her head in the latest fashion.

"Dr. Santros, I presume," smiled Marta Sandoz from around a glass of Aldeberan wine.

"Dr. Sandoz," returned Jules. "I thought you'd be hard at work writing a paper on the negotiations or something."

"Not when there's a party to attend," said Sandoz, raising her eyebrows by way of asking who his escort was.

Jules took the hint. "Joan, this is Dr. Marta Sandoz, a psycho-xenologist who was with the negotiating team that met with the Coalition. Doctor, my wife, Joan."

"No need to be so formal, Jules. Call me Marta. Hello, Joan. I understand you're with the Interplanetary Geological Survey? That must be an interesting job."

"It is," replied Joan. "Especially if you're working with a good team."

"Which includes your husband, I understand."

"That's right. Oh yes, Jules, a brandy would be nice."

Jules slipped away to get the drinks and when he returned, Joan and Sandoz had been joined by Manda Mooney. That brought him up short as his hands suddenly began to perspire. Hoping Mooney would keep her flirtations in check, he approached the group.

"Here you go, honey," he said, handing Joan her drink. "I'm sorry, Miss Mooney, I didn't know you were here. Would have gotten you a drink as well."

"That's okay. Need to keep a clear head if I'm going to pick out some eligible male from this crowd."

It didn't help Jules discomfiture that Mooney was wearing a midnight black, form fitting synthsatin dress that left way too much skin available for inspection. She had loosened her wavy red hair so it tumbled in planned recklessness across her bare shoulders.

Jules cleared his throat. "So, you've been introduced to my wife?"

"Oh, yes, and we've been having a delightful bit of girl talk while you've been away hunter gathering," laughed Mooney.

Joan and Sandoz laughed as well, joining in her little joke at Jules' expense.

"What's been the fallout on the diplomatic front following the breakup of the negotiations, Miss Mooney?" asked Jules by way of taking the spotlight away from himself.

"Back to square one. The Coalition is still outraged at the Consortium's supposed duplicity. But that's just a pose. The way the game is played, they put on an act as the injured party and we pretend to believe them and extend our apologies. That dance should go on for another few weeks before the Coalition lets us know what it will take to soothe their ruffled feathers. Then, we'll go through the motions of protesting, they'll soften their demands, and at some point, in the next six months Terran time, we'll meet them on some other neutral world."

"What are they demanding?" asked Joan, fascinated.

"Right now, they want the Consortium to recognize some territory they gained in the Eridani system."

"We won't let them get away with that, will we?"

Mooney shrugged. "We really have no vital interests there so whatever we decide, it'll be a matter of psychological strategizing."

"That's where Dr. Sandoz' psycho-xenology comes in?"

"You catch on quick, Joan," said Sandoz.

"Do you think their outrage about the missing *John Crosse* is faked?" asked Jules. "I mean, did they already know about it but only acted as if they didn't?"

"To cover for an operation they knew about or even conducted themselves? Possibly," admitted Mooney. "If that's the case, the *John Crosse* could be in the hands of the Coalition right now being reverse engineered."

"How likely is that?" Sandoz wanted to know.

Mooney shrugged.

Conversation veered to small talk after that, mostly involving the universal complaints of colleagues, tangles with administration, and the frustrations of balancing a social life with commitments that often took professionals from one end of the Consortium to another. Before it descended to the level of girl talk about marriage and families, Jules managed to maneuver Joan away by the simple expedient of suggesting a dance.

They lost track of Sandoz and Mooney after that and it was agreed to call it a night. On the way out however, Jules did catch sight of Sandoz talking with O'Shea and wondered if Mooney found herself a dance partner.

Outside the hall, Jules called a speedcar and after helping Joan in, called for travel to dome three and home.

Drowsy from the alcohol she'd consumed, Joan struggled to stay awake till they reached their living unit.

She could never hold her drinks, thought Jules.

He leaned back and put his arm around her and she snuggled up against him, resting her head on his shoulder.

"I think I'll just sleep here," she murmured.

Silently, the speedcar navigated its way among the travel lanes progressing from one connecting tube to another, passing through domes five and six and around to dome three.

On the last leg, they entered the final tube connecting to dome three when Jules noticed that in the 'car's rear view monitor the tube seal from dome two had not closed behind them.

That was funny. Safety regulations dictated only one speedcar at a time could occupy a connecting tube. The seal should have closed as soon as their 'car had passed through. Instead, there seemed to be a delay...Jules sat up suddenly, instantly alert. Another 'car had entered the tube behind them.

"What's wrong?" asked Joan, blinking.

"Another 'car is behind us in the tube."

"That can't be. There must have been a computer error that left the seal open..."

"Maybe," said Jules, then "Increase speed."

The 'car started to move faster, racing to the seal at the opposite end of the tunnel. In the rear-view monitor, the 'car behind them picked up speed as well and was visibly catching up to them.

"Faster," said Jules. "Prepare to shut seal to dome one as soon as we pass through. Emergency override code Archimedes."

Ahead, far down the tube, he saw the green lights that ringed the seal turn to a pulsing red.

Now Joan was frightened. She turned in her seat and tried to look behind them, but the high cut of the 'car's canopy prevented a direct sight line to the rear.

"What's happening?" she asked.

"Too much for coincidence. This kind of thing never happens. Two speedcars in the same tube at the same time? At least I've never heard of such a thing before. Considering what happened with the 'dactor, I'm inclined to think that this is no computer trafficking error."

Ahead, the exit seal was growing larger by the second as the speedcar leaped forward. Behind them, the following 'car was moving even quicker, eating up the distance between them with alarming rapidity.

"Rear view," said Jules. "Magnify."

Instantly, the rear-view monitor showed a close up of the pursuing 'car, its blunt nose filling the screen.

"Magnify again, twenty-five percent. Adjust upward fifteen degrees."

The view changed slightly as the angle shifted and the magnified image showed through the plas-glass canopy of the approaching speedcar.

It was empty.

"No one's in that car," said Jules, mentally calculating how many more feet there were to reach the exit seal. He figured there was still another half mile to go.

Nothing more needed to be said as both Jules and Joan realized yet another attempt on their lives was in progress.

"Faster," shouted Jules as the pursuing vehicle completely filled the rear-view monitor.

In a last burst of speed, the 'car seemed to leap for the exit, in a flash passing from the tube into the lane dedicated to the residential sector. Behind them, the seal irised shut and instantly there was a tremendous explosion as the following speedcar slammed into the durasteel barrier rupturing the plas-glass material of the tube and briefly releasing a fireball of pressurized gasses into the thin Martian atmosphere.

Chapter Nine

Grim Discovery

"I don't care if this is an open frequency," shouted Jules into his telcomm. "I want to speak with the director!"

They were in the salon area of the suite assigned for Joan's protection only a few minutes after getting back from dome security where they'd spent an hour telling their story of the runaway speedcar to a group of disbelieving tech officers.

Not knowing how much he should tell them, it was all Jules could do to keep his story straight. He and his wife were simply coming home from a banquet when something apparently went wrong with the traffic computers controlling activity within the travel tubes. The fact that no body was recovered from the other speedcar was no concern of his. All the more reason to suspect a malfunction with the computers.

The security techs were having a hard time buying it, and he didn't blame them.

It was well after midnight when they finally gave up and let them go home. That, however, was not and could not be the end of the story. At the moment, Joan was sitting on the pnuemasofa still shaking and still in tears over the close call that for the second time in a few days nearly took their lives.

"No, I don't want to speak to the assistant director," Jules was saying. "I want Director Leclerc!"

Jules went over and sat down next to Joan, throwing a reassuring arm around her shoulders.

"Don't worry, honey, we'll get to the bottom of this...Director Leclerc? You've heard about the incident in the tube? You know that was no accident. I know what I told security, but what else was I going to do?

Tell them I'm an agent for Military Intelligence on a secret assignment?" There was a pause while Jules listened. "Security has done some looking around have they? What? You're kidding?"

"What is it?" asked Joan, suddenly alert.

Jules placed his call on hold a moment. "Security checked up on the speedcar that was following us and found out that it was registered to Marta Sandoz."

"You're kidding?"

Jules unheld his telcomm where Leclerc had continued to speak. "Look, director, just fix it with security to cooperate with me. Tell them anything you want, but make sure I don't run into any interference. Can you do that? Good. How soon? Okay. I'll wait."

Jules discontinued the call and turned to Joan.

"So far, all Leclerc knows is that the 'car was registered in Sandoz' name. I have to wait for a call from security for any more information."

"I just can't believe Marta was involved in any plot to kill us," insisted Joan. "At the party she seemed so friendly."

"I agree with you but it can't be coincidence. We've got to learn more."

It was about a half hour later when his telcomm buzzed. It was dome security and after identifying himself, Jules was connected with the officer in charge of the crash investigation.

"Yes, sir, Doctor, the 'car was registered to Marta Sandoz who took possession at the same address where the diplomatic banquet is being held. Officers are in the process of questioning attendees about anything they know of her movements since leaving the site."

Jules had no idea what Leclerc might have told dome security about him, but there was no indication at all of reticence on the part of the officer he was speaking to.

"In addition, we are in the process of tracking down for questioning anyone who may have left the banquet early, but so far, we've learned nothing of substance."

"What about Sandoz herself?" asked Jules. "Do you have any idea of her whereabouts?"

"According to the timeline we've been able to assemble, she

arrived at the banquet early and remained on the premises for the entire time except for a few minutes when she stepped out for some reason that no one has been able to explain."

"About when was that?"

The officer paused a bit before replying. "Eleven fourteen p.m. local Mars time. We've been able to pinpoint the time because it was then that she took possession of the speedcar which was automatically registered in her name."

"That was around the time my wife and I left the banquet ourselves," said Jules, lifting a questioning eyebrow to Joan.

Joan nodded.

"Are you suggesting there was a connection?"

"Maybe. What did she do after going outside?"

"She returned to the banquet, only leaving when it was over at about two a.m. Alone."

"Where did she go after that?"

"No one we questioned had any idea. We then checked her suite in dome twelve, but she wasn't there."

"What about the tube that allowed two speedcars in at the same time? Any ideas on how it was done?"

"There is evidence that the traffic computers had been tampered with," said the officer. "Not an easy thing to do. As you may know, they include triple password protection and multiple foiling redundancies expressly to prevent deliberate interference with tube controls. Someone, however, was able to do just that. Evidence of a very sophisticated operation. If the incident was specifically planned as an attempt on your lives, then someone was very serious about wanting you dead. Very serious."

"I...understand," said Jules.

"Which begs the question, do you know of anyone who might do such a thing? Do you have any enemies, business rivals, jealous lovers, whatever?"

"I'll need some time to think that over," evaded Jules. *He'd have to hand that one along to Leclerc.* "By the way, do you have the number of Sandoz' suite? I might go over and look around if security is finished there."

Jules sensed a bit of hesitation on the officer's part before he was given the information.

"Well, thank you, officer," said Jules, concluding the interview. "I hope you'll keep me informed as the investigation continues."

"You can count on it."

Was there a note of suspicion there? Jules wondered. *Well, the officer wouldn't be a professional if he didn't suspect there was more to Dr. Santros than was being let on.*

"Honey, I could wait till later to check, but I get the feeling that the sooner I get to Sandoz' suite, the better," said Jules. "Security isn't informed about my assignment from MI and may have missed something there that they didn't realize was important."

"If you're trying to tell me why you're not staying with me, forget it," said Joan, who was her usual unflappable self again. "I'm going with you."

"But the danger..."

"I'd rather be in danger with you than safe here surrounded by strangers."

"I guess I can't blame you. Let's go."

After overcoming their initial reluctance to trust the speedcar that pulled up in front of the residential complex, it was a short ride over to dome twelve where Sandoz kept her suite. Taking one of the up capsules to level six, they found Suite 609 easily enough. Of more recent construction than dome three, the suites in dome twelve were secured with ID comps keyed to the tenant's flash code instead of a laser key. But a quick call to MI resulted in a remote override that let Jules in with a minimum of fuss.

"Maybe we should have announced ourselves first," said Joan as they stepped into a tidy little foyer. "I mean, what if she were here and was stepping out of the shower or something?"

"Never thought of that," admitted Jules, looking around. "Unfortunately, it's too late to worry about that now."

As they made their way into the main salon, Jules didn't know what he'd expected to find. Would the room be in disarray from a hasty search, bags in the middle of being packed? Surprisingly, there was nothing of the kind. The salon was neat and trim with nothing to catch anyone's attention.

"What are we looking for?" asked Joan, peeking in the bathroom.

"Anything out of the ordinary, I guess. Something that might tell us where she went."

While Joan drifted into the single bedroom, Jules passed through the salon into the kitchen nook. There, everything was clean and in order. No odors of a recently prepared meal. No stray crumbs on the counter. The sink receptacle was bone dry. The 'fridge component stocked.

Back in the salon, Jules began going through in-wall cabinets and peeking under the furniture. The plas-glass floor to ceiling window gave onto a balcony and an excellent view of traffic lanes that looped among the dome's interior structures. Giving up, Jules turned away from the window and joined Joan in the bedroom.

"Find anything?" he asked, glancing over the feminine items one would expect to find in a woman's private chambers.

"No, but I have noticed one funny thing," said Joan, stepping out of the closet she'd been inspecting.

"What's that?"

"Take a look in here," said Joan, motioning to the closet.

Jules went over and stuck his head inside. Except for the vague scent of lingering perfumes there was nothing out of the ordinary.

"Notice anything?"

"She uses Cologne Parisienne No. 5?"

"Very droll."

Jules shrugged.

"The clothes hanging in the closet," said Joan. "The dress Marta wore at the banquet isn't there."

"She wore something in green crinosynth, didn't she?"

"So, you *were* paying attention."

"Cut it out." Jules turned back to the closet and rummaged through the assorted dresses, blouses, and jump suits hanging in there. "No green crinosynth. So what? You're suggesting she never came back here after the banquet?"

"Exactly. Was there someplace else she could have gone?"

"The offices of the Exterior Ministry where she works...unless she went home with someone from the banquet."

"The security officer you talked to said she left alone."

"Right. I have an idea." Jules pulled out his telcomm and spoke a number.

"Hello?" said a voice.

"Miss Mooney? This is Jules Santros."

"Oh."

"I'm calling about Dr. Sandoz. I need to locate her."

"Sorry, I have no idea where she went after the banquet."

"I can't explain, but it's important I find her. She's not at her suite. Is there any place else she might have gone? A friend's...?"

Mooney caught the gist of Jules' suggestion. "Marta and I went on the prowl together a couple of times but we weren't that close. Let me make a few calls and get back to you, okay?"

Jules agreed and put away his telcomm. "Might as well make ourselves comfortable."

He and Joan retreated to the kitchen to see if the brewer was in operation and by the time they'd finished their synth-coffee, a chime sounded indicating that there was someone at the door.

Jules looked at Joan who shrugged. Curious, he asked the suite's computer who was at the door.

"Manda Mooney," came the reply.

"Why did she come here?" mumbled Jules, telling the computer to allow Mooney in.

Mooney smiled as she entered the room, changed now from her black synthsatin dress to a neo-1940s ensemble that had conquered the fashion scene a few years before.

"I didn't expect you to deliver the information personally, Miss Mooney," said Jules, getting up from the sofa. "You needn't have bothered."

"No bother. I couldn't sleep after the banquet. Too much of that Terran gin, I think. Besides, if Marta is missing, I'd really like to help find her."

"I appreciate your concern," said Jules. "I assume you found out something otherwise you wouldn't have come...?"

"I think I did," said Mooney. "I called some of members of the delegation's science advisory team and found out that Sandoz has one of those vacation suites at Planem Boreum."

"I've been there before," said Joan. "Very cozy. They don't call them 'hideaway' suites for nothing."

The Planem Boreum resort area was made possible by the ongoing efforts at terraforming Mars. Warming temperatures due to a building atmosphere began to thaw ice buried beneath a thin crust of soil and dry ice at the north pole, filling fissures and basins with water. That triggered a real estate boom among developers. Soon the shores of the new lakes and ponds were dotted with domelets and in-ground, multi-unit suites perfect for the vacation and layabout crowd.

"You didn't happen to get the address of Sandoz' suite, did you?" Jules asked Mooney.

"I'll share it with you if you let me tag along," replied Mooney.

It didn't take long to register a flyer and soon the threesome was heading to the north polar region. Nothing indicated just how weak man's hold on the planet was than the few minutes it took to outstrip the cultivated regions around Marsport. After that, the trip consisted of hours of travel over empty wasteland and blasted landscapes of impact craters and dead sea bottoms. It was all beautiful in its way, as Joan remarked, with its striations of rust red colors and wind carved formations. It wasn't yet any place people would want to live.

Presently, they approached the northern zone, and suddenly they were in sight of the Marshlands Resort, one of the newer playgrounds made up of ultra-modern suites built directly into the curving slopes of an ancient meteor crater now slowly filling with water.

"Nice," remarked Mooney. "I could take this."

Some dust was kicked up by the flyer as it settled in the resort's private airfield which was dotted with scores of other vehicles including a number of tour-trams that took vacationers for jaunts across the lake and points beyond. Just now, a pinkish sun was coming up over the horizon, accentuating the white native concrete and plas-glass construction of holiday suites that clung to a steep crater wall looming over the landing area.

The information desk in the main lobby was helpful and soon they were walking down a long tunnel carved through the Martian rock, scanning door numbers until they found the one they wanted.

"This is it," said Mooney. "Now what?"

In reply, Jules followed the same procedure he did to get in to Sandoz' suite in dome twelve, and in no time the door to the vacation unit slid open.

"That was easy," said Mooney. "Remind me to call you the next time I forget my laser key."

Much smaller than the units back in Marsport, the vacation suites consisted of a small salon in the center with kitchen nook and bathroom and bedroom wings to either side, all with floor to ceiling plas-glass windows giving a spectacular view of the water filled crater outside. Bedroom and bathroom windows had a polarizing option.

"Take a look around but don't touch anything," said Jules, starting out.

Apparently having the same idea, the women both made immediately for the bedroom and stopped short at the entrance.

"Better have a look over here," Mooney called over her shoulder. "I think we found a clue."

Jules came over and stopped short in the bedroom entrance. The women had stood aside to let him in.

Except for the body on the bed, the room was empty.

The windows had not been polarized so that the rising sun cast everything in a pinkish glow. The garish red coverlets on the bed seemed to soak up the light as did the green crinosynth dress pooled on the carpeted floor. On the bed was a woman lying on her stomach, her long legs stretching past the edge of the isomattress, her arms might have been cradling her head. Her figure was barely concealed in the briefest of nighties.

"Marta Sandoz, I presume," said Mooney calmly.

Chapter Ten

The Plot Thickens

The room was quiet a moment. Nothing moved, like in an old still life painting. So much so that Jules almost expected Sandoz to roll over and ask if she'd fooled them. That, however, didn't happen. Instead, a chill suddenly seemed to creep up from the floor, the chill of a room where all life had fled.

Next to him, Mooney continued to stare at the body and Jules wondered at her lack of emotion, especially of a woman she had known if only slightly.

She'd seen death before.

Joan, on the other hand, was obviously disturbed at the discovery and tried to hide her nervousness.

"A negligee," she noted irrelevantly. "What she's wearing. Didn't think anyone used them anymore."

"Back in style," said Mooney, still staring at the body. "On Earth anyway."

Any other time, Jules might have considered the outfit attractive, but the effect was spoiled by a small pinkish hole in its center, right beneath the shoulder blades.

"Shot by laser gun," he said, leaning over the body to make sure. "Very little blood. The wound was instantly cauterized. A projectile weapon would have been a lot messier."

"And noisier," added Mooney.

"That too," admitted Jules, looking under the bed and then around the room before his gaze fell on a small, scorch mark on the wall over the headstead.

"She was shot in the back while standing up," he concluded. "If she'd been shot while in bed, the beam would have burned through the isomattress to the floor."

"Whoever did it had to have been someone she knew. Otherwise, how did they get past the ID comp?" said Mooney. "Unless she let the person in, they would have had to know the suite's flash code."

"In either case, she must have known her killer," said Jules.

"A lover?"

"Did she have any?"

Mooney shrugged. "She didn't lack for male attention. And a single person doesn't keep one of these hideaways just to come and do some heavy thinking."

"We...I mean, the police will have to look into that. Find out if she ever came up here with anyone."

"The operator of the 'dactor was killed by a laser too," recalled Joan, biting a knuckle.

"I'm not forgetting that," said Jules, looking at Mooney out of the corner of his eye. Would she pick up on Joan's remark? He wasn't sure how much to tell her about his interest in Sandoz and so had kept it to a minimum. Luckily, however, she seemed more shook up at finding Sandoz dead than she let on.

"Should we look around for clues?" asked Mooney. "I mean, isn't that what's expected in situations like this?"

"Use your eyes only," advised Jules. "Don't want anything disturbed for resort security."

They searched the suite then with Joan sticking close to Jules. It didn't take long to look the place over. It was small. When they came together again in the salon, they still hadn't found anything suspicious.

"Whoever it was, did a good job of covering his tracks," concluded Jules. "We'd better leave well enough alone and report the murder to security."

Jules would have preferred to let Leclerc handle it, but with Mooney present, he had no choice but to do what was expected. As a result, he again found himself frustrated by red tape as resort security officers insisted they all stay until every last detail of their business at Planem

Boreum was explained. All he wanted to do was to get back to Marsport and begin his round of visits to family members or acquaintances of the Science Division researchers who took those oh so coincidental leaves. For that, he wanted Joan at his side as protective coloration. An average looking married couple asking questions would seem a whole lot less intimidating than a strange man with nothing but a Military Intelligence flash ID to hide behind.

Luckily, his explanations about his involvement with Sandoz' death managed to satisfy the security officers as well as Mooney thus keeping his MI connection under wraps. Joan didn't have to pretend being shook up by the whole thing because she really was and that seemed to discourage close questioning of her by the officers.

A call to Marsport security by the officers informing them of the speedcar incident also helped to cover his tracks by giving him a plausible explanation for his interest in Sandoz' whereabouts. That seemed to end the questioning, and they were let go with the admonition to leave the police work to properly trained security personnel in the future.

"Yes, officer," said a properly contrite Jules, holding his breath until they were safely away in their flyer.

By that time, everyone seemed talked out and the flight back to Marsport was largely a quiet one with everyone keeping their own thoughts. For his part, Jules was trying to fit the pieces together. Where did Sandoz, an advisor for the diplomatic corps, fit into his search for the missing Science Division researchers? Was she involved in the attempts on his and Joan's lives? It was under her name that the runaway speedcar was registered. Was she knowingly involved in that incident, or did someone only use her name as cover and then kill her to keep suspicion focused on her? Was Sandoz then simply a tool? Did she make the acquaintance of the wrong person who decided to use her identity because she was handy? Was it possible she might have been involved up to her beautiful neck until someone else decided to cut their losses?

Whatever the case was, it was getting serious, really fast. Not that the theft of a Navy battleship wasn't serious enough nor the Coalition's continued use of black hole tech, but now it was personal. Not only had there been two attempts on both his and Joan's lives, but now the circle of misfortune was widening. Other people were being dragged in and actually killed. More than ever he needed to get to the bottom of the mystery before the odds caught up to him and he or Joan ended up like the unlucky Sandoz.

Chapter Eleven

Following the Trail

The whine of the reverse thrust engines jolted Jules to wakefulness as the shuttle entered Earth's atmosphere.

For a moment, he wondered where he was then remembered. Three weeks ago, he had exhausted his leads on Mars and was forced to take his investigation to Earth where all he had to go on was a single name, one of his colleagues from the research labs at Military Intelligence. Faced with the inevitable, he caught a naval cruiser back to the home planet and spent the week in transit worrying about what would happen if he failed to get on the trail of the renegades. To get his mind off that problem, he tried going over his plans for finding Georg Heintzle.

Looking out of the tiny porthole, all he could see were clouds and condensation streaking the plastiscene pane. Giving up, he threw himself back into his seat and closed his eyes.

After attending the diplomatic fete and eliminating Clyde and Kadaka from suspicion, he'd spent his last days on Mars running down the addresses to their missing fellows. That wasn't hard to do since for the most part, they lived in government housing within the Military Intelligence dome. A few, though, had suites in other domes, preferring to stay away as much as possible from the more regimented atmosphere of the MI dome. Luckily, they didn't prove to be too far away, just a speedcar jump to one of the residential domes including one in dome three where Jules and Joan had their own suite.

Jules smiled, remembering how he'd brought Joan along with him to check out the local addresses. The dash of domestic camouflage worked like a charm, only it proved unnecessary as they found the suites either abandoned or occupied by others. Family members who knew nothing about the plot in any case had been sent away. There were no forwarding addresses.

Of course, Joan was disappointed to hear he would have to leave her again and she would have to go back into protective custody, but what was he to do? The fate of the universe hung in the balance, or so he told her.

"I don't think any husband ever had the nerve to use that kind of an excuse to get away from his wife," Joan complained.

"You believe me, don't you?" Jules asked, tongue in cheek...of course, you never knew...

Luckily, Joan was the understanding sort, helped him pack his things, kissed him on the cheek, and sent him on his way. It was that kiss on the cheek that worried him. He was sure she'd been more shook up by the attempts on their lives as well as the discovery of Sandoz' body than she let on. Sure, she didn't like his going on alone, but she hadn't put up much of a fight either.

There was a bump as the shuttle hit some turbulence and broke through the clouds to emerge somewhere over open water. Jules only assumed it was the Pacific Ocean since they were due to land at the space port outside Reno.

Anyway, Georg was the only member of the missing researchers Jules had been unable to investigate directly on Mars. His work with the agency ended months before the other leaves were granted, and he'd moved back to Earth to take up residence at his last known address, a suburban unit in the high country outside Joshua Tree, California.

If that lead didn't pan out, it was back to the computer console for hours of tracking down extended family members of all the missing researchers in hopes one of them might have heard from their wayward relatives. Jules didn't relish that and dearly hoped something came about through Georg, whom he remembered as being roughly his own age, an expert on gravimetrics and white dwarf parameters recruited from SoCal Aeroflotilla Laboratories which happened to be located outside Joshua Tree.

The red warning lights came on, and Jules prepared for landing which did not come soon enough for him. Minutes later, he was exiting the shuttle into the bright Nevadan sunshine, happier than he expected to be in an atmosphere that did not require breathing enhancements o r protective outerwear.

He was directed to a terminal building where he was cycled through with a minimum of fuss. Outside again, an escort in military tans led him to a private field where a number of rocket planes sat on the tarmac.

"Headed over the mountains I hear?" asked a civilian pilot, his eyes hidden behind a pair of opaque sunglasses.

"You my ride?"

"If your name's Jules Santros, it is."

"That's me. Which one's your 'craft?"

"None of these horse and buggies," said the pilot. "Follow me."

He led Jules on a short walk to where a row of corrugated hangers sat baking in the sun. The first in line had its big doors open with the pointed nose of a sleek rocket plane poking out.

"This one's mine," said the pilot unnecessarily. "The latest model plus some improvements by yours truly."

"Fast?" asked Jules, grateful for the cool shade inside the hangar.

"Won the high desert speed trials last two years in a row. Why? You in a hurry?"

"Could be. Where do I stow my gear?"

"There's room behind the passenger seat," said the pilot, taking Jules' bag and stuffing it in back of the rear jump seat. "Get in."

Jules did so. He let the pilot fix the safety straps and adjust his helmet and oxygen mask. Satisfied, the pilot hopped into the forward seat and wasted little time lowering the canopy."

"Tower, this is AR-2, read?"

"Read," crackled the receiver.

"Ready for take off. Special delivery."

"That's a roger, AR-2. Special delivery."

It seemed his arrival had been prepared for because the plane was quickly cleared for takeoff, and in no time the pilot maneuvered it into position at the head of the runway.

"You are cleared for takeoff, AR-2."

"Roger, tower," replied the pilot. "Better hold on to your breakfast, pal."

The next thing Jules knew, the plane was in the air and climbing at an enormous rate. He hardly even saw the runway as the plane left the field and headed like an arrow into the sky. It seemed the pilot had not been kidding when he said his plane was fast. In fact, Jules barely exchanged more than a word or two with him before he was signaled for an impending descent.

"There's Joshua Tree over there," said the pilot, pointing off to the west. To the east rose the jagged peaks of the Rocky Mountains, many of them snow covered. They hopped right over them by the simple expedient of reaching to the edge of space and then diving straight down.

"Field, this is AR-2 approaching," the pilot called.

"AR-2, we have you and you are cleared to land on runway 6J."

"Roger that."

Jules didn't know if special arrangements were being made for him, but he was grateful not to have to spend more time in the air than he had to. Nothing against the pilot or his 'craft but his stomach could only take so much.

A few minutes later, he was on terra firma again and shaking hands with the pilot.

"You come back now, hear?"

"Sure," waved Jules as he made his way to a nearby robo-cab.

Deciding not to waste any time, he told the 'cab to head to Heintzle's address.

Joshua Tree was still a relatively small town. After much of its population moved to Mars in the early days of colonization, a good part of the rest simply left rather than stay in a virtual ghost town. Later, when Aeroflotilla built its labs in the area, the city was revitalized somewhat as a company town. More of an exo-burb than a true city, Georg's home was a modernistic shell on the outskirts embedded in gardens and thick stands of Aceraceae.

Ordering the robo-cab to stop a way up the street, Jules shouldered his bag and alighted. As the 'cab sped away, he looked around. There were only a few other houses in sight, and those well hidden behind their own screens of landscaping. The street itself was empty. Slowly walking up the sidewalk, he approached the Heintzle home, never taking his eyes off it. By the time he had reached the front walk, he'd still seen no one.

Placing his bag out of sight among some flowering shrubs, he stepped to the door and passed his hand over the alarm sensor. Dimly, he heard a tinkling sound inside then the sense that someone was approaching. He was right. Through the side panes along the front door, he saw a figure move. A woman. She stopped before he could make out her features, hesitated, then moved away quickly.

Instantly alert, Jules dashed around the house, leaping shrubs and weaving around stray palms in an effort to catch her before she escaped out back somewhere. Unfortunately, he was too late. He had just broken through to some open lawn when an aircar slid silently from a driveway, took a banking turn, and hovered quickly out of sight down the street. Who could it have been? Not anyone with legitimate business here, surely?

Still wondering, Jules continued on into the driveway and peeked into the open ended garage stall. There was no other vehicle in sight. Inside, an access door stood against the basement of the house. It was ajar. Confident no one was home, he stepped through and moved cautiously up a short flight of stairs past some hanging garden tools.

"Hello?" he called experimentally. "Anyone home?"

He didn't expect a reply so wasn't surprised when none came.

Completing the climb onto the main floor, he stepped into a roomy entranceway that led to the front door in one direction and a pantry in the other. Choosing neither direction, he crossed the vestibule into the living room.

Indoors, the house revealed itself to be quite modern with a few walls of fieldstone and the rest floor to ceiling clear-plas windows making for an airy, well-lit interior. Overhead, polished wooden beams crisscrossed, supporting the roof, making for a woodsy, outdoorsy feel. Jules liked it. That is, until he noticed the papers and such scattered about.

Obviously, someone had been searching the place. Likely the woman he caught taking off earlier. Slowly, he made a circuit of the house, looking in each room in turn but touching nothing. The only sign that Georg may have been home at all was the absence of travel bags. He was supposed to have returned home, that much was known. So far as he had been able to check, there were no travel or credit records indicating that he had gone anywhere else on Earth. No, if he came to Earth at all, it would have been here. This was his home and his employer, the only other place he could have gone, was nearby.

Having completed a cursory examination of the house, Jules began a more thorough check. Although the bathroom had been cleaned, he found a fresh smudge of toothpaste on the side of the sink...he recalled Georg distrusted the sonic toothbrushes recommended by eight out of ten dentists...and there were some strands of hair...still damp...caught inside the shower drain. That was enough for Jules. Georg had been here all right, and recently.

In a small study nook separated from the living room by a stand alone stone wall, Jules found a fully computerized, multi-function workstation. Floor to ceiling clear-plas windows gave the feeling that the nook was actually outdoors amid the riot of tropical plants that crowded close to the house.

Concerned the workstation's security system would give him a problem, Jules used a pocket de-scrambler supplied him by MI before he left. Handy devices those. In seconds, he had the workstation's system deactivated, and a moment later all the passwords were bypassed as well. From there, it was only a matter of telling the workstation what he was looking for to see if Georg had left anything incriminating behind but...that would have been too easy. He soon discovered his former colleague was as thorough as he expected him to be. Every system in the workstation had been wiped clean.

So. Back to square one.

From a pocket in his suit jacket, he pulled out a nano-card and inserted it in one of the half dozen ports in the workstation's input deck. Instantly, pre-programmed nanites streamed into the 'station's hardware to chase down the wiped information. The information still existed somewhere in the cloud and they would find it...the top secret software wasn't called a cloud chaser for nothing.

Jules judged he had a few minutes before the little buggers would complete their assignment so repaired to the pantry to fix himself a cup of coffee, real coffee, not the synth stuff he had to settle for on Mars. When he came back to the office nook, mug in hand, the information he needed had been retrieved.

Taking a sip from his mug, he asked the workstation for Georg's whereabouts, but to his surprise, it had no record of that.

"Search all your files," ordered Jules. "Even the hard drive if you have to."

Still nothing.

Jules was impressed. Apparently, Georg really knew his stuff. Maybe Ivar gave him lessons? Admiration only went so far because it meant he was at a dead end. What now? Well, there was only one more option. Aeroflotilla. Georg likely had a workstation there, and there was just the chance he might not have been as thorough with that as he had been with his own. In fact, he couldn't have. To have been as thorough as that, he would have had to destroy much of his department's research records since all of them were tied in together as a self-enclosed cloud unit. As dedicated a scientist as Jules knew Georg to be, it was just possible he might not have been able to bring himself to do that.

Going back to the kitchen, Jules was about to place his mug in the thermosanitizer when he stopped. There, etched across the mug in big, fancy lettering was the name 'Lucinda.' *Who could that be?* he wondered.

"Look up the name Lucinda, cross reference Georg Heintzle," he said into his telcomm. Immediately, the information he sought began scrolling down the small screen.

"Bernardi, Lucinda," read Jules. "Formerly Lucinda...Heintzle." *What the hell?* Georg was divorced? That was certainly going to be news to Military Intelligence, which usually did a thorough job of vetting its employees. How did this one slip by? Why didn't Georg bring it up himself?

Of course, divorces were hard to come by and not exactly something to brag about. Nevertheless, it should definitely have appeared on Georg's MI fact sheet. The fact it wasn't raised a red flag.

"Locate Lucinda Heintzle, nee Bernardi," said Jules into his telcomm.

He got lucky. A Joshua Tree address appeared. Not far away.

according to the GPS coordinates.

Aeroflotilla can wait a bit, thought Jules, deciding a visit first to Miss Bernardi was called for. After everything that happened to him so far in his investigation, he felt it was best to proceed cautiously, thoroughly, before taking next steps. Besides, he wanted to make sure about who was in that 'car he saw.

Signaling for a robo-cab, Jules left the house the way he went in, retrieved his bag, and waited a few minutes outside until his ride drew up.

"Sonoma Street," he told the 'cab as it drifted down the road on a cushion of air and the invisible signals from fiber optic cables buried in the smart street.

Chapter Twelve

Hot Pursuit

It didn't take long for the robo-cab to find the address.

Lucinda, apparently, exited her relationship with her husband none the worse for wear.

Sonoma Street was a broad, sun splashed avenue that began with a bit of winding before reaching the crest of a low rise. From there it straightened out into a little valley dotted with modern homes of the rustic variety, constructed mostly with natural material as was the latest architectural style and centered with a modest dome, a feature made popular by off world colonies. The road was lined with native plant species and homes thickly screened with the same, Joshua trees and cactus being prevalent.

As the 'cab pulled up quietly before one of the homes, Jules had second thoughts about not having called ahead but decided it wouldn't have made any difference. Either Lucinda was home or she wasn't. She would talk to him or not. Ordering the 'cab to wait for him, he followed a twisty walkway to the front door and announced himself to the housecomp. He waited there in the midday Southern California heat and studied the cloudless blue sky. Quite a difference from the pink of Martian skies. Maybe he and Joan should think of retiring here someday.

"Who is it?" asked a voice from the housecomp annunciator.

"Jules Santros, an old colleague of Georg Heintzle's," said Jules. "Am I speaking to Miss Lucinda Bernardi?"

There was no reply. Instead, the door swung silently open on electronics provided in every smarthome. Just inside stood a woman of middle age and faded beauty. Jules could tell that at one time she possessed a certain exoticism but time had dulled her features. Today, her face indicated she had gained some weight and her dark hair was piled atop her head and wrapped in a colorful scarf. Her figure was softened in loose fitting day clothes.

"Miss Bernardi?" asked Jules.

"Yes, won't you come in?"

Jules did so and stepped into a nicely appointed salon where clear plas windows let in plenty of that California sunlight.

"You said your name was Santros?" asked Lucinda.

"That's right. Georg and I worked for the same...company, on Mars."

"How did you find me? Did Georg...?"

"Oh, eh, no, when we worked together, I wasn't aware he was even married, let alone...well, divorced."

"Then how did you...?"

"Well, that's a bit of a story. Suffice it to say the company we worked for is interested in finding Georg, who seems to have disappeared on them."

"Good luck finding him," said Lucinda, sitting down and motioning for Jules to do the same. "He didn't bother to let me know when he came back from Mars. I found out by accident when I learned he'd returned to his old job at the plant."

"Aeroflotilla?"

"That's right. When I found out he was back, I went to find him and we talked. It wasn't the kind of conversation you'd expect from a former husband to his former wife, no matter the circumstances of their splitting up."

"Do you mind if I ask you why that happened? It's something he never informed our employer about after they completed a background check prior to hiring him."

"It's simple enough."

To Jules' relief, Lucinda didn't seem too bothered by about the divorce. "He wanted that job badly. Something about black holes and he really wanted to be in on it. I wasn't ready to move to Mars. I had a good job here with Aeroflotilla and like living in the southwest. Having to live for years maybe under domes and having to breath air through masks and 'tubes...well, that didn't appeal to me at all. Anyway, he insisted on going and we ended up with a divorce. He was angry at the time due to the delay in leaving for Mars, but what can you do? The government doesn't make it easy for couples to split up. You need a good reason. Luckily, we had a good lawyer and managed to get the preliminaries done in a few months. After that, Georg could go off planet and the process could continue without him."

So technically, Georg had still been married when the background check was likely to have been conducted.

"When you finally saw him again, it was only after he recently returned from Mars?"

"Um hm."

"It wasn't a warm welcome?"

"Hardly. Talking with him, I had the distinct impression he was in a hurry. Wanted to get rid of me. Now don't you think any normal man would at least have a friendly word to say to his ex-wife? Ask her how things are going. Does she need any help? Maybe even meet her for dinner or something."

"If their parting was on friendly terms."

"It was. No hard feelings."

"So, you only saw him that once I take it?"

"Yes. I'll admit I thought about trying again but before I could, he left."

"Do you know where?"

Lucinda shrugged. "No."

"Do you know if Georg met with anybody else while he was here? I mean besides fellow employees of Aeroflotilla?"

"Not that I know of. I don't think he was here long enough to socialize with anyone."

"Has anyone else besides me been around asking for Georg?"

"You're the only person."

That's good, thought Jules. It meant he must have beat that mystery woman here.

"By the way, Miss Bernardi, you didn't happen to be visiting Georg's home about an hour ago did you?"

"No. Why?"

"I went there first and saw a car leaving the driveway just ahead of me. A woman was inside."

"A woman? I don't think Georg has been back long enough to have picked up a girlfriend," said Lucinda, smiling. "By the way, what exactly was the name of this company you work for?"

"Well, it's not a private company, it's the government..."

"Oh, now I get it."

"What do you mean?"

"Your being vague about who you and Georg work for, all the questions, the mysterious woman in the car. It all adds up. The government never tells us everything it's up to."

"Well, the war..."

"Even if there wasn't any war. I don't care. Keep your secrets...and Georg if you can find him."

"Maybe someone up at Aeroflotilla might know where he is," said Jules, rising.

"Can't hurt to ask," said Lucinda noncommittally. "It was nice to talk with you, Mr...Santros was it?"

Jules nodded before heading to the door.

"I appreciate your cooperation, Miss Bernardi."

"Good luck, Mr. Santros. With whatever it is you're up to."

"Yes. Well..."

Jules wasted no time making his exit from the Bernardi residence and little more before he began to think over some of what he'd learned. For instance, how did Georg know he'd be working on black hole technology when he was hired by the Science Division? No one was supposed to know about that prior to receiving a triple-pass top secret clearance, something that was not earned until a deep background check had been completed and at least six months of employment observation. All new employees knew upon being hired was that they would be working on highly sensitive projects for the military. Did Georg have inside information? Was there a leak in Military Intelligence somewhere? Was the apparent plot by Georg and the others planned far in advance? Up until then, Jules was under the impression whatever the renegades were up to, it was something they cooked up while on the job with MI. With this new information, he was being forced to conclude the plot might go far deeper than that.

Further ruminations on the matter were cut short when Jules noticed a familiar aircar parked on a side street running along the far side of the Bernardi lot. He could only see the top of its canopy above the heavy landscaping, but the color was definitely familiar. It was the same 'car that pulled away from Georg's home earlier in the day.

Since Lucinda said she received no other visitors asking about her ex-husband, Jules guessed whoever was in that car was not going anywhere but waiting for him to leave so she could go in herself.

Quickly, he slid into the front seat of his waiting robo-cab and gave it orders.

"Swing around and enter the first street on the left," he said. "Take it easy."

Immediately, the 'cab pulled away from the curb and swung around in an easy U turn that brought it directly in line with another side street that ran through the neighborhood opposite from where the mystery 'car was parked.

"Down here. Now take the first left and stop at the end of the street," ordered Jules as the 'cab approached a cross street and turned left. About three hundred yards further along, the street ended where it met the side street on the other side of the Bernardi home. "Stop." The 'cab halted. "Now move up slow until I say to stop." The 'cab began to move forward slowly until Jules spotted the mystery 'car where it was still parked up the street to the left. "Stop."

Jules craned his neck to get a better look but could only confirm that the 'car was occupied.

"Okay, pull out to the left and come up alongside that aircar."

The 'cab turned slowly left and drifted quietly up to the other 'car. Jules was looking forward to seeing who the occupant was but before his 'cab was completely in position, the other 'car began moving and pulled away.

Spotted. "Follow that aircar," he shouted to the 'cab. "Don't lose it."

Instantly, he was pressed against the seat as the 'cab increased speed to keep up with the other 'car which was increasing the distance between them very quickly.

"Scan license tag and search registry," he ordered. "Who is that vehicle registered to?"

There was barely a delay between the time it took for the 'cab's sensors to read the aircar's identifying signals and report its findings. "Regina Gogowski, resident San Francisco, date of registry..."

"Stop." The name meant nothing to Jules. Likely an assumed one.

Now the aircar led them back onto the main smartway and with its speed still increasing, surprised Jules by switching lanes. He became even more surprised when it changed lanes again. Now it was on the farthest lane to the right, the one reserved for slower moving delivery vehicles, before hovering onto a side street at the last minute.

"Turn right, turn right." His commands were too late. The 'cab had already passed the street where "Regina" took her 'car.

Damn. The only way she could have done all that was if she disengaged the 'car's smartway controls. Jules didn't think anyone knew about that. Not the average person anyway.

Well, he wasn't exactly average himself.

"Override command Delta service plus," Jules told the robo-cab. "Security matrix seven twelve alpha. Designation SD/MI."

There was no discernable delay before the 'cab acknowledged the override passcode and a manual joystick sprung from its hidden recess directly between his knees. Taking the stick, he looked around and shifted lanes. Shooting ahead of a lumbering airlorry, he scooted into the next right-hand street.

The last-minute maneuver didn't come without some swerving, startling a motorist coming from the opposite direction. It would take a few seconds to get used to driving manually. How long had it been since he had last driven an aircar himself? Jules didn't have time to do the calculations as he struggled to keep the 'car under control while increasing its speed to maximum safe allowances. He had to catch up with "Regina" or whoever she was.

Quickly gaining confidence at the 'stick, Jules took another right turn, hovered up the street, and shifted left again onto the next parallel smartway, the route "Regina" took earlier. As he increased speed, he expected to catch sight of her 'car at any moment. Having taken that turn earlier and likely seeing his 'cab overshooting it, she probably figured she lost him. Sure enough, he soon came into sight of the powder blue aircar in question.

Suddenly, it picked up speed again. She'd spotted him. Jules increased power to the turbines and shot ahead himself. What followed was a dizzying chase with Regina's 'car shifting from one lane to another and attempting to place other 'cars between herself and pursuit. As required by smartway regulations, when an aircar began to act erratically, other vehicles were required to stop until the danger was passed. Such stoppages in effect placed roadblocks in front of Jules that he had to avoid, forcing him to slow down and lose ground.

She's done this before, thought an admiring Jules. That reminded him of a similar thought he'd had before but could not identify at the moment. *No time now.*

Luckily, his old manual driving skills came back to him and he was able to avoid a crash with the halted vehicles while keeping "Regina" in sight. Ahead, she took another turn and moments later, he followed finding himself on a narrow two lane smartway leading into the open desert. It twisted and turned while trending upward into the hills. Now barriers appeared along the edge of the road where the hills sloped away steeply and Jules began to wonder if the smartway would end somewhere ahead.

The chase led onto a lengthy straightaway, and Jules could see they reached a good height overlooking a valley that at least *looked* pretty far down. It was then the blue 'car disappeared around a sharp turn. Jules immediately judged he was traveling too fast to hold the curve. He tried to slow down but it was too late. The 'cab swerved and fishtailed into the roadside barrier, damaging the rear thruster and effectively putting him out of the running.

Ahead, he could see the blue aircar continuing downward trailing clouds of dust left in the smartway by desert winds. Cursing his luck as well as his rusty driving skills, Jules canceled his passcode and told the 'cab to call emergency service, but sirens in the distance more than likely meant that he would have to deal with traffic police before help arrived.

Chapter Thirteen

Trap!

It did not take long to reach the outskirts of town where homes thinned out amid increasing woodland. Slowly, the ground rose in the direction of the nearby mountains that loomed overhead as strange and awesome as any alien landscape. But before they drew any closer, the robo-cab slowed and pulled up to a gate set in a metal fence stretching off to either side of the road. A sign read:

SoCal Aeroflotilla Laboratories
Joshua Tree Campus.
Private property.
Fence monitored by satellite.

Jules had little time to think about what to do next before an aircar approached the gate from the opposite side. In it were a pair of uniformed security guards.

Getting out of the 'cab, Jules met one of the guards at the gate.

"Can I help you, sir?" the man asked.

"Yes. I'd like to see the facility manager. It's urgent business." He extended his telcomm that displayed his credentials including the one from Military Intelligence.

The guard examined the information as it scrolled past the screen.

"Just a minute," he said, returning to his vehicle.

A minute later he came back and signaled the gate to open.

"Come in, Mr. Santros. Mr. Minniac will meet you at the head office."

"Wait for me," Jules told the robo-cab before joining the guards in their own vehicle.

They followed a winding road that led up the ridge upon which the main facility was built, and soon Jules spotted a massive structure that towered over the trees that otherwise blocked his view. He recognized it as an enclosed test stand for gravimetric devices, the biggest in fact, he had ever seen. Impressive. The structure disappeared behind mo re trees as he was conducted to a sleek glass and metal building where he was told that director Henrico Minniac was waiting for him.

Sure enough, he was greeted by Minniac in the lobby. They shook hands.

"You've come a long way, Dr. Santros," Minniac was saying. "All the way from Mars I'm told."

The comment was meant as an invitation to explain his presence at Aeroflotilla so Jules filled him in.

"As you've been made aware, I've been delegated by Military Intelligence to investigate the disappearance of Ge org Heintzle, who also happened to be a colleague of mine on Mars," no need to tell Minniac anything about what they were doing as colleagues. "He's a suspect in the theft of a naval cruiser from Earth orbit."

The look on Minniac's face indicated disbelief.

"I admit it sounds fantastic, but Military Intelligence can't overlook any possibility," continued Jules. "I came to Earth to see if Georg might have returned to his home here in Joshua Tree and it seems that he has. He wasn't there when I...visited...but there was e vidence that he'd been there recently. His home workstation files had been thoroughly wiped, not something that happens by accident."

Minniac agreed it was unlikely.

"I understand Georg visited his office recently?" Jules pressed.

No need to tell Minniac anything about his visit with Lucinda Bernardi, formerly Heintzle.

"He did, but how did you...?"

"Good," said Jules before the director had time to continue. "I got the idea information on his workstation here might still exist. Any little detail could be the key I'm looking for."

"Well, I guess you have to investigate every possibility in business like this," conceded Minniac, affixing a visitor's badge to the lapel of Jules' suitjacket. "Follow me and I'll show you to his office."

It was not far. A pleasant up capsule ride took them into the upper levels of the administration building. On the seventh floor, Jules stepped into a large open area filled with rows of workstations occupied by busy secretaries doing whatever it was secretaries did. Around the circumference of the room were conventional doorways obviously leading to separate offices.

"Here we are," said Minniac, holding a door open for Jules. On it was a plaque that read *Prof. Georg Heintzle.*

The room was modest in size, but Jules could tell that the multi-function workstation was the best money could buy. A wall of clear-plas windows allowed a beautiful view outside, downslope over the forest to Joshua Tree in the distance.

"When was the last time Prof. Heintzle visited this office," asked Jules, recalling the fresh toothpaste in Georg's bathroom.

"A few days ago," replied Minniac. "We were expecting him of course. We knew he was due back from his trip to Mars. He sent news ahead to have his laboratory prepared to set specifications in anticipation of getting right to work. I don't mind saying that we missed his input around here while he was working for the government."

"He *is* a brilliant man," admitted Jules. "Do you know where he went since he was last in?"

"I wasn't aware that he'd gone anywhere," said Minniac. "I thought he was at home."

"Is there any place you know of he might have gone other than his home?"

Minniac paused a moment to think. "No."

"You're aware one of your employees is his ex-wife and lives here in town?"

Minniac looked uncomfortable. "Lucinda does work for us."

"What about his secretary, his colleagues, would they know?" Jules decided not to press the Lucinda angle since he already knew Georg had not been in contact with her.

"I can ask them."

"Do you mind doing that while I go through his records here?"

"Of course not. I'll be right back."

Turning to the 'station, Jules went through the same procedure as he did at Georg's home, expecting and finding that again, everything had been wiped. Again, he pulled out the nano-card and put it to work. This time he had success.

Information began filtering back into the workstation, building up a record of activity. Finally, there was enough to go on. Jules began with the most recent entries and worked his way backward. Jules caught a break. Because his records would be tied in with the facility's own mainframe, Georg had not been able to do as thorough a job cleansing his files as he did with his home 'station. Not without seriously compromising the facility's own records, something he obviously did not want to do. Which indicated however he was involved in the theft of the naval ship, Georg may not have been as committed to the plot as at first assumed. That gave Jules hope.

"Let's see," he mumbled to himself as information cascaded on the embedded screen before him. "Lab records, flow charts, survey findings, research notes, business trips, aircar records, flight itineraries, five-year plan, equipment orders..."

Jules stopped. Could it be this easy?

"Director mechanics for deep space navigation!"

That was the phony heading military intelligence had given their research into black hole tech. Why had Georg listed it here? Quickly, Jules navigated through menu options, tracking down the files listed under the phony heading. It all boiled down to Test Stand 1. It was there he would find the answers.

Dashing from the office, Jules found Minniac was nowhere in sight. Deciding not to wait on him, he received directions to Test Stand 1 from a girl at one of the workstations, leaving word with her to tell the director where he went.

Passing from the room, he stepped into an enclosed catwalk connecting the administration building with the labs on the other side. A long corridor led to a down capsule at the end which took him to a sub-tunnel giving entry to main electronics and mechanical assembly. His company issued badge allowing him passage with no questions asked. Finally, he arrived at Test Stand 1, the same massive structure he had glimpsed on the road outside.

At the moment, the test stand was not in operation, apparently it being between experiments. Aeroflotilla was the largest manufacturer of gravimetric devices in the Consortium and having patented the first artificial gravity systems a hundred years before, continued to lead the field in the development of more commercial applications. In fact, it was one of the largest military contractors, second only to Lockheed, Martin, & Boeing, builders of naval spacecraft.

So maybe it was lucky he was able to find the Test Stand idle...or maybe not. There must have been a reason why Georg created the file with the phony black hole tech project name. Jules walked over to one of the half dozen hatches that gave access to the huge, enclosed space inside the test stand. Peering through the thickened plas-glass aperture, he saw that it was empty; just a vast, metallic floor space. He knew that beneath the deceptive flooring lay a complex array of equipment that controlled, contained, and measured the gravimetric energies released onto the test stand during experiments.

"Can I help you?" asked a lab tech, approaching him from a distant workstation.

"Was just looking. Are you familiar with Prof. Heintzle?"

"Georg? Sure. You know him?"

"I worked with him on Mars."

"You don't say?" said the tech, crossing his arms. "He isn't around today. Was here a couple days ago though."

Interested, Jules wanted to know more.

"Know where he went?"

"He told me he was going home. I assumed he meant his place in town."

"What was he doing down here?"

The man shrugged. "Going over some stats for an upcoming experiment. We're...by the way, have you been cleared to be down here?" He glanced at Jules' ID tag where it hung on his suit jacket.

"Call director Minniac and check for yourself."

"I'll do that." The man took out his telcomm and beeped the director. Minniac's voice came on. "I have a Mr...Santros down here, Doctor. He's asking questions, but I wanted to make sure he had clearance before I answered them. He does? Fine. Guess you're all right."

"So, what was Heintzle doing down here?" Jules asked again.

"Well, he was picking up where he left off when he went on sabbatical to Mars," said the tech. "At the time we were working on dwarf-matter experiments..."

"Dwarf-matter as in white dwarfs...collapsed stars?"

"That's right. The company has managed to manufacture dwarf-matter artificially...not an easy process, believe me...and we've been experimenting with it for about two years now trying to find just the right amounts needed for different jobs."

"In space, a white dwarf is formed from the triple-alpha process," said Jules. "Fusing helium to carbon and oxygen."

"That's right," agreed the tech. "If not enough heat is built up to fuse the carbon, it combines with the oxygen to form a heavy mass which as you say, in space would end up being the remains of the dead star...one whose mass after millions of years could further collapse into a black hole."

"And Georg's experiments?"

"Well, handling the artificial carbon-oxygen fusal mix, as you must realize, is a lot easier than doing it with a black hole. If it could be properly controlled, there's no limit what that gravimetric power could be used for..."

"I get it. Did you notice any unusual action or requests from Prof. Heintzle?"

The tech thought for a moment. "No, nothing. He spent some time in the test stand, but I can't tell you what he was doing there."

"Mind if I look around in there?"

"Nope. Nothing to see though." So saying, the tech went over to the hatch Jules peered through and punched in a code on a touch pad in the wall. Pretty low tech so far as security systems went, but then who would want to break into an empty test stand?

As the hatch hissed open, a message came through the tech's

telcomm. He answered it.

"I'll have to leave for a few minutes. Be right back."

Jules did not wait for the tech to get out of sight before stepping into the test stand. Just inside the hatch he stopped and stared. Sure enough, it was the biggest he had ever seen. Most of those he had worked with over the years were never more than half its size.

He took a few more steps farther in, listening to the sound of his feet echoing among the metal plates that covered the structure's interior surfaces. Slowly, then more obviously, he began to notice that his feet became more reluctant to leave the flooring. He had been aboard enough space vessels to recognize the sensation of artificial gravity as it tugged at the soles of his shoes. Rapidly however, its grip increased until he could barely lift his feet.

He lost his balance and fell to his knees then his stomach. The pull was growing more powerful. If it continued, he would not be able to breath, he would be crushed. Straining with all his might, he managed to raise his shoulders to arm's length before collapsing for the final time. Ahead of him, he could see the open hatch, beckoning, teasing, but it might as well have been on the other side of the Moon for all he could do to reach it.

As if an impossible weight descended upon him, he felt his ribs creak and he could no longer draw in breath. He was being slowly crushed to death, and there was nothing he could do about it.

Chapter Fourteen

On the Moon

Suddenly, he was breathing again. Instinctively, he tried to draw in a deep breath before pain in his chest brought him up short.

"Take it easy, tiger," said a woman's voice.

"Breathe slowly, Dr. Santros," said Minniac from somewhere close by. "It'll take a few minutes before your muscles ease up."

"Even then, your ribs are going to be sore for a while," said the woman's voice again.

He was lying on his back, on the floor. Slowly, he forced his eyes open and a woman's face came into focus. It looked familiar.

"Mooney? Manda Mooney?"

"It's me, all right."

"What are you doing here?" Around them, a number of white suited techs looked on curiously. Minniac waved them away.

"Same thing you are, trying to get a line on Heintzle," Mooney was saying.

"If it were not for Miss Mooney, you'd surely be dead by now," said Minniac. "Crushed to a pulp in the test stand."

"I spotted you coming down here, followed, and when I saw something was wrong, called Dr. Minniac here," explained Mooney.

"It was only luck that I was on my way down at the time," continued Minniac. "As soon as I received Miss Mooney's call, I ran the rest of the way. I realized what must have happened, of course, so wasted little time initiating emergency measures."

"What...what did you...?"

"The dwarf-matter is susceptible to intense heat...one of the problems we've been working to overcome to make it commercially useful. I super-heated the carbon-oxygen mix, it was only a few molecules held in a special chamber beneath the test stand, and that lessened the gravimetric forces enough to drag you from the chamber."

"A little CPR after that did the trick," finished Mooney.

"You...?"

Mooney nodded. "Just part of the training."

"What training?"

"I'm an agent for the Exterior Minister's office."

"A spy?"

She laughed. "If that's how you want to look at it. It doesn't do any harm to tell you now, since my cover's blown," said Mooney. "O'Shea assigned me to investigate the stolen navy ship. See, the minister's office doesn't fully trust the military to investigate itself, so once they found out that you'd narrowed the search down to just Heintzle, they sent me ahead of you to check up on him."

"Then it was you I saw in Georg's house? You're Regina?"

Mooney caught the reference at once. "I am. I used that name to register my aircar. That was a good chase you gave me on the smartway, by the way. I haven't had my driving skills tested like that in a long time."

"Thanks, I guess."

"Anyway, after you fell behind, I turned back to keep an eye on you since the purpose of my coming to Earth was no longer valid. I followed you here, got inside, and when I saw something was wrong in the test stand, called the director for help."

"How did you get inside the facility?"

"I'd like to know that too," said Minniac.

"I'm a secret agent, remember? That's my job."

"Ouch," Jules cried, as he tried to get to his feet.

"Take it easy," said Mooney, helping to steady him. "It's going to hurt for a while."

"It must have been a trap," mumbled Jules. "Georg set me up. Thought for a while there he might not be fully in with the other renegades. Sure was wrong on that count."

"A trap?" asked Minniac, startled. Clearly the thought had not occurred to him. "You mean Prof. Heintzle deliberately tried to have you killed?"

"Not me personally," replied Jules. "Anyone who came snooping after him. He couldn't wipe all his workstation records without damaging the facility's own research records. If he did that, it would have left a big footprint signaling anyone that something was up. So, he did the next best thing. He left a false clue pointing to the test stand. Anyone stepping into it would set it off. I was just dumb enough to do that. By the way, doctor, I'd have your techs check out the below decks arrays. Likely whatever it was that triggered the trap when I stepped inside the test stand is still functional."

"I'll get them right on it," said Minniac, rising.

"It was only luck that no one else had a reason to go in there before I showed up," said Jules.

"Well, looks like this is a dead end so far as tracking down Heintzle is concerned," sighed Mooney. "Maybe if we go back to his house and..."

"No use," said a rapidly recovering Jules. "His home workstation was thoroughly wiped. All the files were...wait a minute! The files!"

"What files?" asked Mooney, startled at Jules' sudden outburst.

"The ones on Georg's workstation! He didn't wipe them all out. There was something there that I think might be useful."

"Boy, you don't ease up at all do you? Here you are with maybe a few cracked ribs and..."

"Can't ease up. There's too much at stake. Help me up." Jules took hold of Mooney's arm and let her haul him to his feet.

"Ow. That hurts, but don't stop. Take me over to the lab tech's workstation."

It took nearly a full minute to cross the room where the tech who he'd first spoken to upon coming down to the test stand rose from his chair and held it out for Jules.

"Thanks," said Jules, lowering himself gingerly into the chair. "This 'station ties in to all the other workstations in the facility, doesn't it?"

"If you know the passwords it does," said the tech.

"Give me the sign in window," Jules told the 'station. When it appeared, he gave it Georg's password. "Now give a list of Professor

Heintzle's files."

Instantly, icons began to stream past the screen. "Stop. Open the file labeled aircar records."

Opening, the file displayed a complete history of Georg's use of the company's fleet of aircars. "Scroll to the latest entry," ordered Jules even as the data jumped to the final log.

"Bingo," said Jules excitedly. "Ouch!"

"What is it? What did you find?" Mooney wanted to know.

"Apparently, Georg didn't own his aircar. He relied on company vehicles for use around the neighborhood. This last entry shows he used a company aircar not two days ago, about the last time anyone saw him. It went to the municipal rocket field outside Barstow."

"Now we've got something to go on."

"What do you mean 'we?'" asked, Jules twisting in his seat and inadvertently sending waves of pain through his sides.

Noting the wince on his face, Mooney replied, "You think you're in any condition to do any pursuing on your own? Besides, it'd be pretty silly for us both to be running around after Heintzle separately, wouldn't it?"

Holding his side, Jules gave it some thought. Two heads would be better than one...if he could forget how pretty the one on Mooney's shoulders was.

"Okay," he agreed. "We work together."

"Good," said a pleased Mooney. "Now let's get you to the infirmary. If you don't get those ribs taped up, you won't even be able to walk out of this place."

A half hour later, they were in Mooney's aircar speeding along the smartway to Fresno.

"So, O'Shea put you up to this?" Jules was asking as they sat back and let the 'car do the driving, or rather, the smartway.

"He didn't put me up to it," replied Mooney. "He's my boss. Head of ministry security."

"So, you weren't a real secretary?"

Mooney laughed. "You think I can't do two things well? Sure, I wasn't the minister's real secretary, but I could do the job. And I was doing it at the negotiations. You didn't notice?"

Jules realized she was flirting again but tried to ignore it. Maybe it was something she did instinctively, to every guy she met. "I did. I was fooled, wasn't I?" Then, "How long have you been on the case? Since the reception?"

"Before that," said Mooney without volunteering any more.

"So, you knew more than you let on that day we found Sandoz at the resort?"

Mooney shrugged.

"That was good acting," admitted Jules. "Better than your pose as a secretary."

"Thanks."

"Did you say the ministry doesn't trust the military?"

"In a general way, yes. You have to admit that the Navy has good reason to hush up the theft of one of their ships. That's pretty embarrassing."

"I guess so. And did you find anything in Georg's house before I got there?"

"Not much. There was some dirty laundry in the autochute. The laundrymech hadn't been turned on in a couple of days, so I knew he'd been around."

"Didn't think to look there..."

"You're a man, silly."

Jules smiled, thinking that was something Joan had been likely to say.

"Nothing else?"

"His workstation was wiped. That alone let me know something was up but nothing else."

"Was that when I broke into your little investigation?"

"You sure gave me a start. I didn't expect you to get there so quickly. Thought you were someone from Aeroflotilla come looking for their employee. Soon as I saw it was you, I got out of there as fast as I could."

"You move pretty fast when you want to," admitted Jules.

Mooney shrugged, her tight-fitting leisure wear flattering her figure. Jules noticed it was made of the new light absorbing stuff, so its black color would make her virtually invisible under low light conditions.

"You have any ideas for when we get to the rocket field?" Mooney asked.

"Check the register, I guess. Speak of the devil. There it is now."

As the smartway unwound ahead, the hills around them flattened, giving way to an arid plain in the midst of which was the rocket field. They were still miles away, but even from that distance, they could see at least two commercial liners resting in their cradles and the cluster of administrative and passenger processing buildings off to the side. A control tower for local rocket planes poked up from behind a few hangars down field.

"Better report in to O'Shea," said Mooney. "Let him know where I am."

Jules barely heard her speaking into her telcomm. His mind was racing ahead, figuring out different possibilities, where to look in case the register idea didn't pan out.

A few minutes later, the aircar slid to a smooth halt in front of the passenger processing center and settled to the ground. Jules and Mooney wasted little time alighting and making their way to the registration desk.

Impressed both by Jules' MI identification as well as Mooney's ministry security ID, the desk manager wasted no time in displaying the passenger list for the waiting rockets. No luck.

"What about other flights over the past couple of days?" asked Jules.

"There was one North American/UK spaceliner that lifted off two days ago," said the manager, barking orders to his company telcomm. "Here's the passenger list."

Jules looked and scanned down the list. Suddenly his eyes widened. "That's the one. Where was the liner headed?"

"Alpha Centauri," said the manager.

"What about the next rocket off planet? When does it leave? Where is it going?"

"Flight 712 leaves in a few hours. It's scheduled for a stopover on the Moon before heading out to Callisto."

"Callisto..." mused Jules. "A resort colony mostly, isn't it?"

The manager nodded, guessing Jules' intentions. "You should still be able to catch a connecting flight to Alpha Centauri from there. It's one of the more popular routes."

"Then get us aboard flight 712."

A short time later, Jules was strapped in to a seat in the coach section of the liner, Mooney beside him.

"I'm not used to this," said Mooney. "I mean traveling coach."

"Oh, that's right," said Jules. "You're government property. First class all the way."

"Hey, you are too."

"We lowly scientists never get the royal treatment you people in the ministries do."

Further conversation was cut short when a red light flashing overhead indicated that the pilot was prepared to cut the ship's gravitic anchor. That would be followed a few minutes later with ignition. Sure enough, the rocket shuddered beneath them and so smoothly that they hardly felt it, the huge bulk of the commercial spacecraft began to lift past the cradle harnesses that even then were still in retreat away from the upright rocket.

Suddenly, the true G forces of liftoff began to tell, and Jules felt himself sink into his conforming seat. There was a moment of nausea that passed quickly, and in seconds the rocket had reached the stratosphere and in a few more, freefall. It was then that main engines kicked in, boosting the rocket from near Earth orbit on a trajectory to the Moon. Soon, the vague roar of the engines ended and Jules knew it was simply a matter of coasting to their destination. One that he could not arrive at soon enough.

"What's our layover at the Moon before moving on to Alpha Centauri?" asked Mooney after recovering from liftoff.

"Six hours," said Jules. "Too long."

"Can't be helped. But once we leave the Moon, it won't be long before we get to Alpha Centauri."

Jules did some mental calculations. "Will a week be too long? We have no idea what Georg plans to do once he gets there."

"With luck, he'll likely be using the same name he registered with at Barstow...by the way, what was the name he registered under? You recognized it pretty easy."

"You won't believe this..."

"Try me."

"Marta Sandoz."

"I don't believe it."

"Told you."

"What nerve. Do you think he had anything to do with her murder?"

Jules shrugged. "Actually, he signed in as Manda Sandoz, but still..."

"I guess that settles the question of how alert those clerks are at the ticket counter. Why would he use her name though?"

Jules shrugged. "I have no idea. It would seem strange for Georg to use a name someone might recognize though."

"Unless he were feeling cocky. His lack of house cleaning back in Joshua Tree would indicate that."

"Recklessness can work to our advantage. Let's hope that's the case."

Just then, another signal light indicated that lunch was served, and as they picked what they wanted from the menu display, Jules lapsed into silence. Mooney seemed all out of small talk and that suited him fine. He was getting to like her...a dangerous thing for a married man. Thought of Joan reminded him that he had not spoken to her since leaving Mars, and she hadn't been happy at the time about going back into protective custody. Digging out his telcomm, he put in a call to Mars Central.

"Joan, just Jules calling in to let you know I'm all right," said Jules, taking into account the three hour delay the call would have in being received on Mars. "Left Earth but can't say where I'm headed next. Hope to see you soon. Love you."

"Too bad."

"What's that?"

"Too bad you're married," said Mooney. "Any woman would be more than happy to have a man as loyal as you are...or seem to be?" she finished on a hopeful note.

"Joan is one heck of a woman."

"She'd have to be, obviously. You won't mind if I keep trying, do you?"

Jules tried to avoid noticing the way her eyes twinkled when she said that.

"Who you calling now?"

"My boss at Military Intelligence."

This time Jules used the encrypting function and texted his report. No point in letting Mooney know everything he was about. He finished t he message with a request that Leclerc message ahead to Alpha Centauri naval command giving him clearance for whatever help he might need.

Finished, he concentrated on his meal and tried to ignore the fragrance of Mooney's hair.

The layover at the Moon went more quickly than anticipated, and the big ship was able to move on in a good deal less than six hours. Next stop, Callisto, a popular honeymoon destination for Centaurans, something Jules learned from Mooney who spent some little time talking it up over the long days out to Jupiter.

Chapter Fifteen

Callisto

Jules was wakened from a nap by the dull tones of the ship's anunciator, signaling a message from the pilot's cabin.

"Attention, passengers. We are now entering the orbit of Jupiter. Please return to your seats and engage gravitic harnesses. As you know, Callisto is the outermost of Jupiter's four moons and as such does not experience the mean motion resonance that the inner moons do with the mother planet. However, the Jovian system's celestial mechanics being as complex as they are, approaching Callisto is always a little tricky. Our approximate arrival at Artemas Colony will be in about four hours. Thank you for your cooperation."

There was the usual excited mutter among the passengers at such news, something that proved contagious.

"Almost there," said Mooney, with a smile in her voice. "Wait till you see Artemas Colony. The name doesn't do it justice."

"It's just another vacation spot," insisted Jules, knowing that his cavalier attitude would only encourage the woman's enthusiasm. "You've seen one, you've seen them all. Food, swimming, gaming, and more food."

"Of course, but this is Callisto. It's not just any old resort getaway. The pools are fed from an underground ocean and warmed by the light of Jupiter itself. You can swim from one pool to another over a hundred square miles of domed protection. Ever hear of the jungle pool complex? For the right price, you can spend a week in there without ever meeting another human being. Just swimming and lounging under the foliage with that big colorful planet hanging over you like a huge balloon."

"For at least a couple weeks at a time," reminded Jules. Like most moons, Callisto showed only one face to Jupiter at all times. He had to admit, that jungle complex sounded interesting...with the right company of course. Looking at Mooney, there was no doubt she would be that kind of company. It was with difficulty Jules reminded himself that he had someone he was crazy about waiting for him back on Mars, and in protective custody at that.

Mooney waved her hand in dismissal.

"So, you plan to use the jungle complex when Jupiter is overhead," she said. "There's still something to be said about the jungle at night, when Callisto passes behind the planet. Picture it when Callisto comes out of its shadow and the sun comes up again. Beautiful."

"Okay, I'll admit it sounds nice."

"There's the nightclubs, the restaurants, casinos, tours of the inner moons, the fast 'cars and slow dancing at the famous Lounge," continued Mooney. "I won't even mention the fully equipped honeymoon suites where I'm told some couples stay and don't come out for weeks."

"You sure you don't work PR for the resort in your spare time?" asked Jules, not liking where Mooney was taking her travelogue. He was saved further discomfort by another announcement from the pilot.

"As we prepare to fire retro-thrusters, passengers are encouraged to watch their seat monitors for a good view of our final approach to Callisto."

Jules waved his monitor on, hoping his action would prevent Mooney from continuing her hard sell.

Instantly, an image of Callisto's brownish face filled the screen as the moon, almost the size of Mercury, grew larger quickly with the action of the liner's thrusters. In no time, Jules was able to make out its craggy surface, one of the most battered in the solar system, where it was not obscured in wisps of carbon dioxide of which its thin atmosphere was composed.

That was all right because Artemis Colony, as cities were on Mars, was protected by a dome. In this case, the largest free-standing dome anywhere in the Consortium. One that covered almost one hundred square miles of the Callistan surface beneath which were the resorts, famous or notorious, depending on your point of view, throughout a dozen star systems.

"There it is," pointed out Mooney as the dome gleamed in the reflected light of Jupiter that hung in the background like some huge, unreal beach ball.

It was an impressive sight, Jules had to admit. Made of the strongest polymers in the plas-glass family, it offered a completely unrestricted view of Jupiter and its other moons in the sky overhead. And as they drew closer, he could make out structures that here and there dotted the thick canopies of landscaping and white ribbons of smartways that swooped among the different regions of the resort. Constructed within a chain of ancient impact craters, the dome was anchored by a series of steep ridges thrown up by meteors that must have struck as a group millions of years before.

Now Jules caught the glitter of open water dotting a jungle of plant life taken from every corner of the Consortium and fed by pumps that brought up water from the moon's buried oceans. Suddenly, the sound of the thrusters changed pitch and passenger seating began to realign as the liner assumed its vertical landing position. On the monitor, Jules saw the forest of gantries that marked the colony's rocket port grow quickly as the liner came in for a landing. Everywhere, rockets of all types sat upright in takeoff position or lay in cradles for servicing. Tiny vehicles darted among them while enclosed passenger debarkation slidewalks moved thousands of eager vacationers efficiently through terminals with a minimum of delay.

"Impressive, isn't it?" asked Mooney.

"We're just passing through," Jules reminded her.

"We have eight hours before our connecting flight. Time to look around a bit."

That's what I'm afraid of, thought Jules as a cradle just below them disappeared from the monitor and the final rumble of landing told him they had reached the surface. Immediately, as with passengers anywhere in the Consortium, everyone stood up at once trying to get their carry-on bags and hurry to the exits.

"Looks to me like these people can't wait to start their fun," observed Mooney.

Amid the tumult, the pilot's voice was saying something over the annunciator, but no one heard him. Waiting until the rush had passed, Jules allowed Mooney to lead the way from the cabin and onto the enclosed passenger catwalk to a down capsule in a nearby gantry. The ride to the bottom was swift and a slidewalk moved them efficiently into one of the busy port's six terminals. Inside, they were ringed by shops and restaurants while overhead, suites were available for business people or travelers making connecting flights. For everyone else, a grand concourse led directly beneath the main dome.

"You know, I just got an idea," said Mooney, heading for the information desk where dozens of uniformed hostesses were answering questions and pointing out the various attractions of Artemas Colony to eager visitors. "It might be that Heintzle had no intention of going on to Alpha Centauri. Maybe that was just a ruse and his real destination was right here on Callisto."

Wary that Mooney's intention was a ploy to get him inside the resort, Jules had to admit the idea made just enough sense to make it worth checking out.

A station at the counter opened up, and Mooney was quick to move in.

"We're looking for some friends who were supposed to be here before us," she told the young hostess. "Could you look them up and tell us what suite they've taken?"

"Certainly," said the hostess. "Who are you looking for?"

"Manda Sandoz."

The hostess repeated the name to her computer.

"Yes. A person by that name is registered."

"Bingo," said Mooney, winking at Jules.

"The party is registered to Suite 2041, building sixteen. We call it the Red Spot resort. Is there anything I can help you with?"

"No, thank you."

"He's here," said Mooney as she and Jules walked away from the information desk and headed for the line of aircars awaiting passengers outside the terminal.

"It appears so, but don't you think it's all a little too obvious? Even signing himself in again as Manda Sandoz? I smell another trap like the one back at Aeroflotilla."

Mooney's enthusiasm cooled somewhat. "You're right. It is too pat. But can we afford to ignore it?"

"Unfortunately, no," said Jules holding the door to the aircar open for her. "Let's check it out fast, because I think we'll still have a rocket to catch when we're done."

Mooney gave the aircar the building number and all they could do at that point was enjoy the scenery which was quite appealing with its variety of buildings done up all in clear-plas and gleaming white foamacrete and swathed in lush landscaping filled with every kind of colorful flower.

If you had to spend a couple weeks honeymooning, thought Jules, *this would be the place.* Of course, he had found a mapping expedition to the Rigel system just as pleasant when he and Joan had combined business with pleasure during their own honeymoon.

Those pleasant memories were cut off as the aircar halted before a towering foamacrete building whose twenty floors were studded by balconies festooned with creepers and crawling ivy dotted with blue flowers.

"Manda must be the romantic type," said Mooney, craning her neck. "He took the penthouse floor."

Stepping across the busy lobby, they entered an up capsule that swiftly took them to the twentieth floor. There, the spacious corridor was empty of foot traffic and tastefully appointed with mood generating stereopticals.

"Fancy," remarked Mooney, scanning the numbers on the doors. "Here it is. Number 2041."

"Hold it," warned Jules. "Let's take it slow."

He motioned for Mooney to stand off to the side, out of the way of the door opening. As she did so, a small hand laser appeared in her hand. *Where did she get that?* Jules wondered.

"Hello, we'd like to see Manda Sandoz," Jules told the suite comp. He felt ridiculous asking for the pseudonym when it was Georg he expected to find inside. Maybe the suite comp hadn't been programmed to recognize any other name. In any case, it made no reply.

"Is Georg Heintzle in residence?" Jules tried again when the suite comp failed to answer to Manda Sandoz.

Still nothing.

"What now?" asked Mooney from where she stood, back to the wall.

"We override the suite comp," said Jules, pulling out his trusty telcomm. He contacted the resort's mainframe and punched in his MI passcode. With barely a discernable delay, he was recognized and number 2041's suite comp overridden.

"Open the door," Jules told the 'comp.

Immediately, the door slid aside, but Jules did not enter. A cool draft of air wafted from the room beyond. Warily, he leaned forward for a better look, but the view did not improve. The suite was completely empty of any kind of appliance or article of furniture. The clear-plas windows on the far side of the salon showed the huge bulk of Jupiter outside, its famous red spot nearly filling the entire view. Even the floor was bare of any kind of carpeting or isotexture.

"Anything wrong?" Mooney wanted to know.

"Not sure," said a cautious Jules. "Pretty frigid in there though. Like the climate controls have been shut down."

"Well, we can't stay out here. We have to investigate. I'll back you up."

"Okay. Keep your eyes open. Something's not right here."

Tentatively, Jules stepped into the room, shivering slightly as his body adjusted itself to the change in temperature. *Must be about forty-five degrees in here*, he thought. Sensing Mooney's presence at his back, he moved farther in. Still nothing. Doorways gave access to other rooms on the right and on the left, a short corridor likely led to bedrooms.

"I'll check the kitchen and lavatory areas, you check the bedrooms," said Jules without turning.

"Right, I—"

Mooney had no time to finish what she was saying because suddenly there was a shudder beneath their feet and an instant later, Jules could have sworn he saw the floor around the edges of the salon shift and wave. Then he was positive when all at once, the floor turned to a kind of liquid and began flowing toward the center of the room, toward them.

"Get out," shouted Jules, turning to shove Mooney toward the door.

Unfortunately, he was too late. The liquid covering the floor contracted toward them, swooped up and over and in seconds they found themselves in darkness, enclosed in a giant metallic ball.

Chapter Sixteen

With a Honeymoon Like This...

"What just happened?" demanded Mooney whom Jules could not see at all so utter was the darkness inside the ball.

"I think I know, but don't ask me how Georg was able to do it," replied Jules, running his hands along the ball's inside surface. He did not have to reach very far to find it.

The ball itself could not have been very big. Large enough to stand in, but its curving surfaces were such that he and Mooney could not stand apart. Jules tried to steady himself by stretching out his arms in opposite directions, but Mooney found herself crowded against him by the slope of the ball's inside curvature. He felt her hands upon his body as she used them to keep herself standing, and he found himself thinking that her nearness was not at all unpleasant.

"Maybe if I used my laser..."

"Don't. It wouldn't do any good and might end up doing us more harm if the beam was reflected off the curving surfaces."

"What makes you think that?" asked Mooney as a dim light suddenly lit the darkness. She was using the screen of her telcomm as a light, and what it revealed did not lift their spirits any. Sure enough, they were enclosed within a black, featureless sphere of shiny metal hardly more than five or six feet in diameter. "If this thing is as airtight as it looks, we're going to suffocate in pretty short order."

Once again, Jules admired the girl's coolness under pressure. She'd faced these kinds of situations before. He recalled the first time that thought had occurred to him. It was after they'd discovered Marta Sandoz' body back on Mars. Now he understood why. In her career as...what? Secret agent? Private investigator? She likely *had* seen it before and also been forced to drive an aircar without benefit of smartway control.

"Let me sit down a minute." Jules hunkered down and pulled out his own telcomm. If he recalled correctly, research on nitinol done by the Science Division before he quite confirmed that the material was signals permeable, allowing the use of standard telecommunications equipment aboard Navy ships. Hopefully, that still held.

"You seem to know something about this thing, whatever it is," Mooney said, sitting down herself and playing her telcomm light around their metallic prison.

"It's a shape memory trap," said Jules, manually inputting commands into his telcomm. No point saying them aloud for Mooney to overhear. "Another project the Science Division has been working on."

"Shape memory?"

"It's a unique property found in metallic alloys composed of nickel and titanium," explained Jules. "Something the division was experimenting with that could be very useful in the construction of space craft, especially naval ships."

"How so?"

"Well, when nickel and titanium are combined, they form an alloy called nitinol that in turn possesses a couple very interesting properties: super elasticity and shape memory effect. Shape memory is the ability of nitinol to undergo deformation at one temperature and then recover its original, undeformed shape upon heating above that temperature. That point is called its transformational temperature."

"You mean this ball is composed of this nitinol stuff?"

"That's right. Just before we became trapped, did you notice how the floor began to waver like a liquid? That was because the room temperature reached the transformational temperature that triggered the change to the nitinol's original shape."

"So, this ball shape was composed out of nitinol first, then allowed to melt down by lowering the temperature in the suite below its transformational temperature?"

"You got it. Do you remember how cold the room was when we first opened the door? Obviously, it was kept that way to hold the nitinol covering the floor in its unformed state."

"Then what triggered the change?"

"It doesn't take much to trip the transformation," said Jules. "If the temperature needed to keep the nitinol in its unformed state was say, forty-five degrees Fahrenheit, then all it would take to make it snap back into its preformed ball shape was our stepping into the room. The introduction of the heat generated by our bodies would have been enough to trigger the change, never mind what residual heat may have entered the room when we opened the door."

"I can see the potential this stuff would have for the Navy," said Mooney. "Constructed of nitinol, any ship that was holed by an enemy warship could repair itself based on the shape memory programmed in nitinol."

"You catch on quick," said Jules. "The problem for the Science Division though is the instability of the transformational temperature. In the cold of space, the nitinol would lose its design shape. But Navy ships have a habit of moving close to suns and very far away from them. The trick was to find that happy spot where the change in temperature would not trigger a change in the shape of the nitinol. The last I knew, that problem was still being worked on by the division."

"Which begs the question, how did Heintzle get enough of it to set up this trap?"

"A good question. Either he had access to a real good lab here on Callisto..."

"Unlikely."

"...or he brought it from Earth or more likely the Science Division labs themselves. One of the renegades is Henry Martine. He was supervisor of the nitinol research project there. With his help, the stuff was probably transported somehow aboard the stolen *John Crosse*."

"Getting hard to breathe in here," noted Mooney, pushing herself away from Jules and massaging her throat. "And colder."

"It'll get colder," said Jules. "I ordered the suite comp to adjust climate control to forty-five degrees and then lower it by five degrees every thirty seconds."

"Is that what you were doing with your telcomm?" said Mooney, elbowing him playfully in the ribs. "Didn't think it could do that. How come you didn't tell me?"

"Does the Exterior Ministry tell MI?"

"Touché."

"Anyway, I guessed the temperature of the room when we first came in was about forty-five degrees. I could have been wrong, but it wasn't much lower than that."

"When it reaches the right temperature, the nitinol will attain its transformational temperature and this sphere will just melt away?"

"Something like that. Of course, we could freeze before then. Nitinol is a good conductor. Another one of the bugs the Science Division needed to work out."

"Maybe if we huddled closer together, we can stay warm longer..." Just then, light broke through the top of the sphere and quickly after that, the dark matter began to recede and in no time melted away and spread across the floor in a large, viscous puddle.

"Just my luck," declared Mooney, staring around.

Jules stood up and offered her a hand.

"I'd say better luck next time, but I'm not anxious to come across another one of Georg's snares," said Jules. "Now c'mon. We have a rocket to catch."

Chapter Seventeen

Distress Call

"Sir," Called the communications officer from his console. "I'm picking up an undefined signal from sector 33A by 16,"

"Can you identify?" asked the XO, Lieutenant Jason Komaki.

"Wait one."

Komaki made his way across the bridge to the commo hut and poked his head in. On a monitor, a sine wave was rolling across the screen in a regular pattern. He picked up an extra ear piece and fitted it in place. Instantly, he heard the distinctive pings that indicated an artificial or man-made signal.

"A distress call of some kind?" he asked.

"Sounds like it, sir," confirmed the commo officer.

"Okay, keep on it, Sparks," said Komaki, plucking out the ear piece and returning to the bridge. "Tracking, key in to Sparks' signal and trace."

"Aye sir," replied tracking. "Got it."

"Coordinates?"

"Tracking. Tracking."

There was a pause while the man fine-tuned his instruments.

"Signal getting stronger, sir," called Sparks.

"I have it, sir. Down range, sixty degrees, sector 33A by 16. Well within the asteroid belt, sir."

Komaki rubbed his chin. Could it be the crew of a disabled ship? It happened before. It could possibly even be an enemy signal of some sort?

"What's the spread on that signal, Sparks?"

"Wide beam, sir. They're not trying to avoid anybody."

"A distress call for sure then?"

"Looks like it."

"Why not use standard distress protocols?" Komaki wondered.

Sparks chose not to speculate.

"Tracking. Can you pinpoint more exactly where that signal is coming from?"

Silence, then: "Sir, there are a number of objects in that sector but the signal appears to originate from Ceres."

Komaki made a quick decision. "Battle stations!" he roared into the ship's anunciator. Immediately afterward, he commed the Captain's quarters. "Sir. We may have a situation developing. Your presence is requested on the bridge."

Minutes later, Captain Rance Montor occupied the command chair and sat, studying an image of Ceres on a drop-down monitor. The largest of object comprising the Asteroid Belt, Ceres was almost six hundred miles in diameter and had gravity enough to force its shape into that of a sphere. For those reasons, it had been classified in years past as a "dwarf planet" and even boasted a form of self-government in the early days of solar exploration when it became an important source of iron and titanium and its mining population grew into the tens of thousands.

That was a long time ago. After the development of the sub-photon drive and Earth's breakout from the solar system giving it access to any number of worlds better suited for mining operations, Ceres quickly found itself obsolete and eventually abandoned. Its modest settlements had been ghost towns now for over a hundred years so receiving a signal of any kind from the little worldlet was unusual.

For its part, the cruiser *Sinai* was on routine patrol within Earth's immediate defense zone when the signal was detected and so obligated to investigate.

"Alert group sector control of our situation and set course for Ceres," ordered Montor. "Standard wartime precautions."

As Komaki relayed his orders, Montor ran a hand through his hair. "No voice contact at all, Sparks?"

"None, sir."

"No telcomms?"

"Apparently not, sir."

Sparks' tone didn't betray any emotion, but both he and Montor knew the highly unusual nature of a situation in which any citizen of the Consortium would find themselves out of reach of a telcomm, one of the most essential elements of modern life.

"Sir, all sensor readings are negative," reported Komaki. "Assume standard orbit?"

"Approved. Sparks, do we have a more accurate source of that signal?"

"Narrowing, sir. Sir, mapping suggests it's coming from Ceres Base, the old mining colony."

Montor considered. Wasn't Ceres Base formed around the mass driver they used to use to send ore toward Earth? He punched up some information from the command comp that confirmed his guess. Right. Ore would be sent to Earth orbit where it was collected by unmanned vehicles and transported either to the Moon to construct the first permanent co lonies there, or to Earth itself. The whole thing struck Montor as inefficient, but he supposed it made sense in those early days of space exploration.

At the moment, he was staring at a close up view of Ceres Base whose pre-dome tech buildings were directly exposed to the airless void. From what he could see, there was no sign of life anywhere among the strictly functional ore processing and residential structures.

"As lifeless as it looks, we have to assume there's somebody down there," said Montor finally. "While I doubt if it has anything to do with the Coalition, we can't take any chances. XO, have Lieutenant Sacker prepare his Marines for a descent."

"Yes, sir," replied Komaki.

"You will accompany them."

"Yes, sir."

"Sparks, you heard from control yet?"

"Just now, sir. The say if there's no indication of enemy activity, to investigate but proceed with caution. Units twelve and twenty-one will be re-tasked to our sector."

"Very good. Acknowledge that order."

"Yes, sir."

Meanwhile, Komaki donned his EVA gear and joined the company of Marines as they lined the interior of the assault shuttle. Making his way through the compartment, he took his place at the front of the line, across from Sacker. Activating his gravitic harness, he nodded to the lieutenant who signaled the pilot that all was in readiness and in a moment, the rear hatch slammed shut.

There was a quick jolt, and the next thing Komaki saw from an overhead monitor was the shape of the *Sinai* receding rapidly from view. There was no sensation of movement after that until thrusters were engaged, easing the rugged vehicle into Ceres' weak gravity well. Altogether, it was a short ride and in no time, the shuttle was settling on a long disused landing apron. They had barely touched down, however, when the rear hatchway fell open, gravitic harnesses were released, and the troops moved out as quickly as their bulky EVA suits allowed.

By the time Komaki emerged from the shuttle, the Marines secured a perimeter around the landing apron and engineers gathered beside the hatch leading into the settlement which consisted of a number of bulky structures and out buildings that had all the appearance of having been added piecemeal over the years. There was no apparent damage anywhere so if power could be restored, there was no reason why the buildings might not be reoccupied.

At the entrance, an engineer was waiting for Sacker to approach before hacking into the settlement's ancient computer system to get the main hatch open. Komaki was amazed to see actual wire leads connecting the engineer's hand comp with the door's control mechanism.

This place is *old*, thought Komaki.

Apparently, the engineer knew his stuff, because in short order the hatch door rolled aside and Sacker, laser rifle at the ready, led the way inside. Komaki followed behind another pair of Marines, and the group moved ahead cautiously to the next door. With a half dozen soldiers crowded into the airlock, the outer door rolled shut again as the engineer prepared to conduct the same opening operation with the inner door. His efforts proved unnecessary as the hatch opened by itself.

Inside, Komaki was relieved to find not a squad of Coalition troopers ready to cut them down but a score of men in uniforms of the Terran Navy. They were all smiles and eager gestures as they gathered around and motioned for the Marines to remove their helmets.

"Are we glad to see you," were some of the first words Komaki heard after he took off his helmet.

"Who are you?" he asked when the excitement had finally subsided.

The answer took Komaki by surprise. They were crew members of the stolen *John Crosse*.

Chapter Eighteen

Near Miss at Proxima

Jules sat comfortably in his seat aboard the connecting liner waiting for word from the pilot that they had achieved free fall. Next to him, Mooney dozed, calm as always. He could not sleep. He couldn't keep thinking about that nitinol trap and the other attempts on his life since this whole thing began. They seemed to fall into two categories; either clever, science-based snares or more traditional convenient accidents and shootings. He wasn't sure if the difference meant anything. Should it?

His thoughts didn't have time to go any further than that as the liner pulled away from orbit around Callisto and ignited its main thrusters, taking the ship beyond the plane of the ecliptic. Once it was a safe distance away, the sub-photon drive could be safely engaged and finally and truly start them on their way to Alpha Centauri.

Four-point thirty-seven light years from Sol, the Alpha Centauri system, part of the constellation Centaurus, is actually a binary star system with its twin suns orbiting each other. But Alpha Centauri was only the system's popular name. The Terran colonies to which Jules was headed were actually located on worlds circling Proxima Centauri, a nearby sun with a dozen planets. Two of those, Proxima 4 and 5, were sufficiently Earth-like to have made them attractive as potential settlements and indeed, outside of Mars, they comprised Earth's oldest colonies.

Outside the orbit of Proxima 5 was an asteroid belt similar to the one surrounding Sol between the orbits of Mars and Jupiter. In one of the larger of those barren rocks was the Proxima Naval Station, the largest navy yard outside the Sol system and one of the most sensitive areas in the entire Terran Consortium. It was there most naval shipping returned for repairs and upgrades while many others were built from scratch in its massive slipways. On constant watch was an entire fleet of war craft, four full squadrons on permanent station in addition to a fifth squadron assigned to protect the two colony worlds themselves.

"Ever been to Alpha Centauri?" asked Mooney, using the common designation for the Proxima colonies.

"A couple times," answered Jules, tired and more than a little stiff after two full days stuck in his seat and still suffering an occasional twinge from his ordeal in the test stand. He would be glad when Alpha Centauri's twin suns finally came into view as passengers were told they would a few minutes before. "My wife, Joan, and I outfitted there before heading out in a deep space survey ship for the Interplanetary Geological Survey."

"Really? That's interesting. I thought you were a physicist of some kind..."

"I am, but Joan's a xeno-biologist and I was tired of what I was doing at the time and signed on to keep her company on the mission."

"And saved the universe while you were at it," finished Mooney with not a little admiration in her voice.

"You heard about that, did you?"

"Part of our briefing before those negotiations with the Coalition."

"Of course."

The warning klaxon sounded then, alerting passengers of imminent emergence of the liner from hyper-void and in another moment, the twin suns were in view.

"Impressive sight," said Mooney, watching a screen on the seat back in front of her showing the liner's forward view.

"You never said if you'd been here yourself," pointed out Jules.

"I was born on Proxima 4."

"You don't say?"

"Sub-photon engines off," called the pilot's voice over the cabin intercom. "Passengers will be aware that we are switching to thrusters for the remainder of the trip. On behalf of the crew, I hope you've had a pleasant journey and choose Xinhua-Orient for your next holiday run or business trip."

With that, the intercom went silent and the liner quickly passed the giant Alphan suns and entered the Proxima system, headed directly to

Proxima 5.

Arriving, the liner proceeded to land on the planet's surface, reversing its position and falling through its atmosphere stern first. The roar of the air outside could be heard distantly through the reinforced tintinabulum hull as Robinson City, capitol of the first and oldest colony in the system, came into sight on Jules' seat back monitor. Close to the ground, as its designated cradle came into view, growing larger as the liner approached the ground, the gravitic anchor was brought into play, helping to guide the big ship softly into place.

Later, in the terminal building, Jules hefted his travel bag, admiring the view outside the expansive clear-plas windows where a long rank of spaceliners stood in their cradles diminishing with distance. Overhead, a green tinged sky dominated by Proxima's sun almost but not quite outshone one of Centauri's suns that at the moment hung low over the horizon.

"Come on, Jules," said Mooney, interrupting his reverie. "You've seen rocket liners before."

"I guess I have," admitted Jules as he turned to follow her to the terminal's information counter.

Arriving there, the manager conducted them into his office whose windows overlooked the rocket field outside including the ship from which Jules had just disembarked.

"I've been informed of your arrival, Dr. Santros and have instructions to help you out in any way I can," said the manager.

"Good. I'm trying to find a Professor Georg Heintzle who might also be traveling under the name of Manda Sandoz."

The manager's eyebrows rose slightly at that but he said nothing. Instead, he spoke to his work station, calling up the registration records of the past few days.

"Nothing here under either of those names. I'm sorry."

"Can I look at the registry?" asked Jules. "Maybe he used another name that I might be able to recognize."

As the manager stood aside to let Jules behind his workstation, the air outside was suddenly filled by a crackling sound followed immediately by a huge explosion that rocked the terminal and threw them to the floor.

Stunned, Jules was the first to recover and looking out the window, saw where the rocket he arrived on had been resting in its cradle, there was only a thick pall of oily smoke and raging fires threatening to spread the resultant chaos to the rest of the landing field.

Chapter Nineteen

Assault on an Asteroid

"Cut the gravitic anchors to the *Constitution,*" cried Commander Polditz desperate to regain control of the situation.

"But sir, it's still in the slipway," returned the frightened lieutenant.

"To hell with that," said Polditz, slamming his fist on the big red knob that cut the gravitic anchors. "Better it's damaged some getting free than being caught in there like a fish in a barrel."

"Sir," reported the lieutenant, "the *Constitution*'s starting her thrusters."

"Good," said Polditz, relieved. "Captain Hidatsu guessed what we intended. He's got to get out of there and join the fight."

Even as they spoke, the *Constitution* roared from the slipway, scraping its surfaces against the stone walls from which it was carved and damaging its hull and much of its sensor array but managing to emerge with all its guns firing.

"Patch me in to Captain Hidatsu," ordered Polditz even as he tried to keep track of the other action taking place all around the naval station.

It all happened so fast. One minute everything was operating smoothly, a typical day at the Proxima slipways. There were three ships in various stages of construction, two light cruisers and a battleship with the *Constitution* a nearly completed fourth. In fact, it was slated for official commission in only a few weeks' time. Cover squadrons at their regular duty stations reported nothing amiss. Then suddenly, from nowhere, slipway number three was destroyed in the flash of an ion borer and amid the subsequent explosions, sensors indicated that they were under attack by a Coalition Strike Force.

With half its sensors knocked out of commission, there was no way for Command to tell just how great was the force ranged against it, but reserved military hyper-wave communications, protected in hardened arrays, conveyed the order: all vessels converge on the naval station and fire at will.

Another explosion rocked Command with such concussive force that it knocked most everyone from their chairs. In a rage, Polditz clawed back to the communications console and forced himself to remind all ships not to target the enemy's amidships.

"All ships," called Polditz, "target enemy thruster housings only. Targeted lasers only. No pulse cannons. Repeat, no pulse cannons." Turning to his fire control crew working the defense shield embedded in the asteroid itself, he repeated his order. "Damn it. Targeted lasers only."

"But sir," pleaded a lieutenant, "our whole defense grid is based around the pulse cannons. If we can't use them, we might as well defend ourselves with pea shooters."

"Then do it," growled Polditz, hoping the incoming squadrons could arrive in time to save the yards.

Meanwhile, the explosions eased off and the Command's sensors that were still operational indicated they had the *Constitution* to thank.

Appearing as they did well inside the defense perimeter of the facility's cover squadrons, the enemy ships were able to strike suddenly without fear of retaliation by other warships for some minutes. As such, the last thing they expected was a fully armed battleship to emerge from a slipway and give battle. As a result, Captain Hidatsu caught them unawares, damaging two cruisers and a battlewagon in his first volleys. That bought him enough time to clear the slipway and turnabout, presenting his bow and smallest profile, to the remaining members of the enemy Strike Force.

"Sir," shouted the lieutenant manning the sensor array. "The *Constitution* is firing its bow guns point blank to the battlewagon's broadside...hit, sir."

"Take it easy, lieutenant," soothed Polditz, conscious of the fact that a number of his staff were newly graduated from the Naval Academy. Well, they would be veterans after this. "Just follow the action and keep me posted."

"Yes, sir."

Secretly, however, Polditz was relieved at the news. The yards could not have taken much more of that pounding. As it was, they were likely to remain off line for months while repairs were made. Suddenly, a deep rumble passed through Command like an invisible wave of force.

"Sir, enemy cruiser hitting us with a vibra-drone."

Remaining outwardly calm, Polditz ordered crews outside to find the 'drone and disarm it before it shook the asteroid to pieces. The steady vibrations in the deck were canceled out by a roar heard even through the mile of rock beneath which Command was buried. From experience, Polditz knew at least a cruiser sized warship had been destroyed. He did not know which would be worse, one of his own or a Coalition vessel along with its dangerous black hole technology.

"Sir, *Constitution* reports the *Calvary* destroyed, sir."

A cruiser then. One of his own. Polditz was silent for a moment but only for a moment as the reports continued to come in of *Constitution*'s valiant stand and the status of the nearest cover squadron as it bore down on the yards.

"Sir," called the lieutenant manning the sensor array, "more of our sensors are coming on line and indicate one of the enemy cruisers has abandoned the formation and is moving off."

"Direction?"

"Heading toward Proxima 5, sir," came the reply after some hesitation.

Aware of his duty to protect the civilian population first, Polditz did not hesitate to order the *Constitution* to give chase. Now it was in God's hands. With the destruction of the *Calvary*, they were defenseless against the remaining Coalition vessels.

Slowly, the pounding of the asteroid began to build up again, and Polditz noticed that the vibrations in the deck had not diminished.

~ * ~

The *Constitution* sheared off, firing her port guns as she did so, giving the besieging enemy one last salvo before pulling away sunward on full thrusters. Captain Hidatsu had no hope of catching up to the enemy cruiser before it reached Proxima 5, but he could at least keep it from conducting a sustained assault on the defenseless planet after its initial attack.

Firing ahead, the ship's targeted lasers did little good in impeding the enemy's progress. Whatever its purpose in attacking Proxima 5, it was determined not to let anything sway it from its mission.

"Jefferson," called Hidatsu from the command chair, "are our cold fusion 'casters on line?"

"Yes, sir," replied his XO. "They haven't even been tested under controlled conditions yet, let alone field tested."

"Be that as it may, warm them up. They're the only thing that might have a chance of reaching that ship at this distance while leaving their amidships undamaged. If there's anything we can do to save lives on Proxima 5, we've got to do it."

"It's a hellofa situation sir."

"You got that right, Jefferson."

It was another twenty minutes before the 'casters were ready and when they were, Hidatsu wasted no time in giving the order to fire.

"Direct hit, sir," said the XO. "Missed the amidships by two standard units."

"Damage report?" The enemy vessel was still moving sunsward and not returning fire.

"Damage to enemy thruster flanges, sir, but its engines are still firing."

"Prepare for another shot."

Before the 'casters could be fired up again, the enemy ship arrived within range of Proxima 5 and engaged its weapons toward the surface.

"More speed," called Hidatsu, leaning forward in his chair.

The *Constitution* bore down and as it finally came in laser range, a number of its forward guns opened up, wrecking the enemy thruster housings and forcing it out of orbit. It had time for only a single shot at Proxima 5, and Hidatsu breathed a sigh of relief at that before the cruiser suddenly vanished.

"It must have engaged its black hole drive, sir," said Jefferson, looking over the shoulders of the ship's navigators at the sensor readings.

"Very well, full about," ordered Hidatsu. "Maybe we can still do some good back at the yards."

"Full about," ordered the XO. "Full power to thrusters, gun crews, on the alert."

As the ship's Klaxon's sounded and the *Constitution* prepared to plunge into battle again, the battle came to an end as abruptly as it began. The Coalition task force simply vanished back to where they came from just as the first Terran covering squadron made its appearance.

In Command center, Polditz permitted himself to relax, easing muscles that had been tensed up from the time of the first strike.

Even though the Terrans managed to hold their own and even thwart the enemy's plans, the surprise attack had been devastating. If the Consortium could not do anything to counter the Coalition's clear technological advantage, Earthmen would find themselves confined once again to their own little Sol system as they had been before the invention of the sub-photon drive.

Three hundred years of progress wiped out in a few months. It was unthinkable, but it would happen if nothing was done to even the playing field. What everyone wanted to know was what *was* being done, what *could* be done to, in effect, put the genie back in the bottle?

Chapter Twenty

Into the Unknown

On Proxima 5, the plas-glass windows of the terminal building held against the explosion, but the resultant pressure wave had not only thrown almost everyone inside to the floor but scattered loose objects through the air like deadly missiles that luckily, only caused minor injuries.

As Jules recovered his wits, he became conscious of the sounds around him; alarm klaxons and sirens filled the air. Slowly, as people dusted themselves of debris and rose to their feet, excited voices were raised all around.

Outside, emergency flyers sprayed foam composed of aluminum hydroxide over the area of the explosion to keep fires from spreading to nearby cradles. The chemical foam had great heat absorption qualities that would cool hot metals, leaving a residue of alumina as a protective coating. On the ground, crews dressed in foil coveralls likewise sprayed a gel composed of huntite and hydromagnesite that would decompose under heat turning to both water and carbon dioxide.

In the meantime, thick clouds of oily smoke curled into the green sky, a grim reminder of all that was left of a once proud space faring liner.

"What happened?" asked Mooney, as Jules helped her up. "Was it a fuel leak, do you think?"

"Impossible," said the manager, straightening his chair and throwing himself into it. "We employ the latest safety measures."

"That was no accident," said Jules, easing Mooney onto a nearby couch.

"What do you mean?"

"That was a concentrated neutrino spread," replied Jules going to the window and looking at the hole that used to be Cradle 6. "It's the preferred method of planetary bombardment by the Coalition. I could tell by the crackling sound just before the explosion. We've been attacked."

"Only the most powerful warships have that kind of capability," insisted Mooney.

"I know. They were after us."

Mooney sat stunned. "All that just for us?"

"The dwarf-matter trap back on Earth didn't work, and we escaped the trap on Callisto," explained Jules. "They must have been informed we were aboard the liner and took no chances with a surgical strike. This time, they tried something more general. Obviously, they assumed we might be still on the liner. A neutrino spread is a targeted weapon. You don't use it at random. That liner was hit deliberately. What it means is they're getting desperate so we must be getting close."

"You said we were attacked?" asked the manager who suddenly grew frightened again. "And they're after you? Then you should go, before they strike again. As long as you're here, the lives of thousands of innocent people could be endangered."

"They're already endangered or haven't you heard? The Consortium has been at war with the Outer Arm Coalition for years," reminded Jules. "Still, there hasn't been a follow-up strike. That's not how the enemy operates. Something must have happened to interfere with their routine..."

"Mr. Stannis," said a frightened clerk appearing in the office doorway. "We need you right away, Janice has been hurt and the baggage handlers are threatening to walk off."

"I'll be right there," said the harried manager who left the office just a tad too eagerly.

After he was gone, Mooney joined Jules at the window.

"You said it was a Coalition weapon," she said. "Does that mean they're involved in this too? They're mixed up with the renegades?"

Jules thought for a moment.

"Not necessarily. If there's an informant on our side feeding them information like the theft of the Navy ship and if that informant was cooperating with the renegades, he could be feeding specific information to the Coalition that they'd be certain to act upon without ever knowing that their actions were serving the purposes of the renegades."

"So, the Coalition is being used?"

"Why not? What reason would they have to stop us? If we succeed in our mission, it would be to their benefit. They'd continue to have the upper hand in the war."

"That begs the question, who knew we were here?"

"It must have been O'Shea," said Jules grimly.

"...or Leclerc," countered Mooney.

"O'Shea was on the scene at the negotiations, remember. And if you'll recall, the enemy only got notice of the theft of the Navy ship just before the meeting. Otherwise, why would they have bothered to attend it at all?"

Jules' reasoning brought Mooney up short.

"I'm trying to figure out why he sent me to Earth then," she said at last. "He said it was because the ministry didn't trust the military..."

"Ridiculous on the face of it," replied Jules. "Who do you think has been fighting and dying in this war all these years? You don't think the Navy is as anxious to find who stole their ship as anyone else is? No, he sent you to run interference. He was hoping you'd either uncover and remove evidence before I arrived, or trip me up somehow afterwards."

"I almost did," said Mooney, recalling how she'd been reporting in to O'Shea right along.

"O'Shea's involvement also fits with something else that's been bothering me," said Jules.

"What's that?"

"The two kinds of threats we've been encountering. On the one hand, these scientific traps like the ones at Aeroflotilla and Callisto and old-fashioned assassination attempts like those on Mars and this latest albeit more spectacular effort right here," said Jules, nodding to the still smoking ruins outside. "They suggest that while Georg has been trying to stop us...or anyone on the trail of the renegades...with his own clever snares, O'Shea has been responsible for the more down to earth incidents."

"If you're right, then Marta's murder would fit O'Shea's MO," observed Mooney. "Nothing fancy about being shot in the back with a laser pistol."

"Considering the way Sandoz was dressed when we found her, it was likely she and O'Shea were more than mere partners in crime."

Mooney shook her head. "That kind of cold bloodedness gives me the shivers."

"Well it's too late to worry about that now," said Jules, turning to the manager's workstation. "Let's see if we can't get a clue to Georg's whereabouts from the port records."

After a few minutes of searching they could still find nothing.

"That's it then, the trail ends here," said a disappointed Mooney.

"What we know of it does," said Jules. "Of course, it doesn't. He must have found some private means of getting off world. It's unlikely the renegades would have gone to all the trouble of stealing the *John Crosse* only to base their operations planet side. Don't forget, the *John Crosse* is an interstellar vessel. Its range is almost limitless."

A second search of private rentals also yielded nothing.

"He must be using a different pseudonym," guessed Mooney.

"If so, the game has entered its end phase," said Jules, leaning back in his chair and stretching. "He has no more need to foil any pursuit or no more opportunities."

Jules went silent for a moment. "No more opportunities. I wonder..."

"Let's see if this unit has access to some stellar charts."

"Stellar charts?"

"Right. Don't know why this didn't occur to me before," said Jules, settling himself behind the workstation.

"What didn't occur to you?"

"Assuming he found a deep space shuttle of some kind, Georg has likely rendezvoused by now with the *John Crosse*. From here, there's really nowhere else to go except back into Consortium space which would seem pointless after the chase he's given us. That leaves us the direction Georg took when he left Earth. Why did he come to Alpha Centauri? He could have gone in any number of other directions but he came here."

"So?"

"So, there's no reason not to assume a direct line from Earth to Alpha Centauri needs to stop at Alpha Centauri. The logical conclusion to reach is he was headed somewhere in this general direction. Why not continue that line outward from Alpha Centauri?

"Show me 3D stellar mapping of the Milky Way Galaxy," Jules told the computer. "Besides, I don't think Heintzle is the kind of guy who'd hang around some place that a Coalition cruiser was due to strike with a neutrino spread."

Just then, a three-dimensional display was projected in the air over the workstation.

"Label local star systems in neighborhood of Sol, Orion arm."

The image reconfigured slightly to indicate Sol and other star systems of the Terran Consortium including Alpha Centauri which lay on the far side of Sol, away from the galactic center.

"Hmmm."

"What are you looking for?" asked Mooney.

"I'm wondering where I'd go if I was a gravimetric engineer and a member of a team of scientists expert in black hole technology..."

"To a real black hole?" guessed Mooney.

"Close, but not quite."

"Then where...?"

"Here, I think," said Jules, indicating a point on the map. "It's pretty far from here though...over five thousand light years at least."

"PER-734?"

"A stellar designation. The prefix means that it's located within the Perseus arm of the galaxy."

"Is it a star?"

"Used to be. It collapsed billions of years ago, maybe soon after the formation of the galaxy. A proto-black hole. Something well short of that but massive enough to draw anything within its gravitational reach which is pretty far. What's happened over the billions and billions of years since its collapse is that it has drawn everything in reach toward it, even the basic component of the universe, dark matter. Over time, it all formed a crust around the singularity's event horizon, in effect creating a natural Dyson's sphere. Really quite remarkable...I doubt there's another such phenomenon in the galaxy or anywhere for that matter."

"What's a Dyson's sphere?"

"It's called that after a twentieth century researcher named Freeman Dyson who postulated the creation of massive man-made megastructures in space such as using matter to enclose a whole star. That way, people could live on the inside surface, warmed by the sun and with virtually unlimited amounts of space to occupy."

"And you say this one's a natural sphere?"

"Right. Normally, black holes that are big enough, like NGC 4889 can be tens of billions of miles in diameter and form an accretion disk of super-hot matter. Formation of the disk reaches a point where its relation to the black hole stabilizes and can even form the basis of a new system complete with stars and planets. The process that created the accretion disk around NGC 4889 is similar to what happened in PER-734. The super massive collapsed star inside has been drawing matter to it long enough for a sphere to form. Joan and I visited it briefly while we were working for the Interplanetary Geological Survey."

"Do you think that's where Heintzle is hiding out?"

"Seems logical. It's more or less on a straight heading from here and its magnetic properties would have been familiar to a group of scientists specializing in the effects of gravity and mass. The chance to study up close the gravitational waves from such a massive object alone would pose an irresistible lure to the renegades. The ability of gravitational waves to bend time and space is what makes use of black hole technology in warships so dangerous."

"How do we get out there? Even I know that no rocket liners ever leave the Orion arm..."

"True. But I've got some influence in high places."

Jules stepped away a moment. He pulled out his telcomm hoping that stellar communications had not been broken by the attack. Neutrino weapons had been known to play havoc with atmospheric signaling.

Switching to the hyper-waveband, one reserved for military use only, Jules quickly found himself in somewhat instant contact with MI headquarters on Mars. There were a few seconds delay in messaging, but he could live with that.

Jules was no telecommunications expert, but he understood telcomms worked on the principle that when messages were sent on the local network, they were shunted into sub-space on the quantum level where pre-positioned nanites picked up the signals and directed them where they were supposed to go. Still, the ability to do the same over interstellar distances was generally assumed to be impossible. That the Science Division cracked the problem some years before was not public knowledge, something Military Intelligence was anxious to keep secret as long as possible. There was no need to burden Mooney with all that.

"Director Leclerc. This is Jules. Aside from almost being killed by a Coalition cruiser, not bad at all, sir...what's that? They did? When? I see. It must have been launched to provide cover for the attack here on Proxima 5. I thought the attack indicated we were getting close but that clinches it. Sir, I don't want to say exactly what my plans are over this signal, but I'll need transportation...armed transportation...that's right. We think alike, sir. I realize things must be getting critical and I'm moving as fast as I can. If it's any consolation, I think I'm closing in, sir. Very well, sir...oh. Almost forgot. You'd better take first ministerial assistant Bentley O'Shea into custody. He's the Coalition informant we've been looking for. I think the evidence is pretty strong, sir. I have no time to explain further, but I strongly urge you to put him on ice. Good. Thank you, sir. Something else? They found the missing crew members on Ceres? Did they have any information...none? All right, sir. Thanks for keeping me informed."

"Are they going to pick up O'Shea?" asked Mooney, after he'd wandered back to her.

"Yeah. You know what? That attack we just had was only part of a larger operation. A whole task force attacked the Proxima yards while our rocket liner was being destroyed. We're getting hot, Mooney."

"Call me Manda, will you? That's what my friends call me."

"I think we'd better keep it formal for now, Mooney," said Jules.

Mooney didn't seem to like that. A frown creased her forehead and her hazel eyes narrowed. The storm soon passed with the realization they were closing in on Heintzle.

"So, did I hear you've arranged some transport for us? It better be something more than a shuttle, because the Perseus arm isn't just a hop, skip, or jump away."

"Oh, I think it'll be adequate. Besides, who said anything about you coming along? I mean, I'm thankful for your help so far, but I think you've fulfilled your obligations in this thing whatever they were. After all, the man who sent you out in the first place is likely a traitor..."

That frown returned as quickly as it had vanished.

"That may be," admitted Mooney. "If you think I'm going to leave now, you're crazy. Besides, you wouldn't want me to stay behind and start talking, would you? Might be a little premature for word to get out particularly if things end badly and the galaxy is destroyed..."

"Don't even think such a thing," said Jules, who considered having her held by local authorities before deciding against it. Not because he thought anyone would believe her but that despite himself, he'd become used to having her around. She was someone he could talk to about the mission without having to fill in the back story.

"All right, you can tag along," he finally said, not without a twinge of guilt regarding Joan. Was he really giving in because he didn't want to be alone on the case or because he was attracted to her? It was a notion he continued to wrestle with for the next several hours until they were picked up by a Navy shuttle and taken off planet.

For Mooney's part, she quickly realized the understatement with which Jules had spoken about providing transportation when she stepped out of the shuttle and onto the deck of the *Constitution,* the Terran Navy's newest albeit somewhat worse for wear battleship.

"I guess you weren't kidding about having influence in high places," she whispered, leaning close to Jules. "This is what I call crossing the galaxy in style."

As the two worked at getting their space legs back, they were led by the XO through a maze of corridors to the fore part of the ship and the captain's ready room immediately behind the bridge. They were allowed to wait only a few minutes before the commanding officer himself appeared.

"Welcome aboard," said Capt. Hidatsu, extending a hand first to Jules then to Mooney. "You must be some VIP's to hold up a battleship while there's a war on."

"Our business is pretty important, captain," said Jules. "Unfortunately, that's all I can tell you for now. I'll fill you in on the details once we're under way."

Hidatsu said nothing, a tribute to his professionalism.

"I understand the Proxima yards were attacked by a Coalition task force?" asked Jules.

"It was. We were still in the slipway when it started. Almost never got the chance to get out."

"Then what I heard is true? The *Constitution* is a newly commissioned battleship?"

"Well, it *is* new. As for commissioned, that's another thing. It has had its baptism of fire, that's for sure."

"How bad are things at the yards?"

"Well, they're not good. Two of three of the slipways are out of commission. Three cruisers have been badly damaged and a fourth destroyed. All hands lost."

"I'm sorry to hear that, Captain," said Jules. "You might be happy to know this mission is likely to help settle the score."

Hidatsu's eyes lit briefly at that before he turned to his XO.

"Mr. Jefferson. See our guests to their quarters then report to the bridge. We'll be getting underway momentarily."

"Aye, sir."

Slowly, the big ship's maneuvering thrusters edged it out of orbit and as Proxima 5 fell away astern, main thrusters came into action adding speed. Outside, repair crews continued to work for a time do ing what they could to bring damaged sensors back on line and fix jammed gun ports. Soon enough, however, they were ordered inside and as the battleship proceeded to exit the system, Hidatsu ordered a series of drills performed to gauge the crew's readiness for battle. And while that was being done, he and Jefferson once again retreated to the ready room to meet with Jules and Mooney.

"I don't think we've been fully introduced, Captain," said Jules. "As you know, my name is Jules Santros and this is Manda Mooney. What you might not know but perhaps guessed, is that I'm an operative for military intelligence, and Mooney here is an agent for the Exterior Ministry."

"We figured it was something like that," said the XO.

"What exactly is your mission, Mr. Santros?" asked Hidatsu.

"Our mission, which includes everyone aboard this ship, is to perhaps save the galaxy, Captain," said Jules simply. "You no doubt have your orders that if engaged by the enemy, you're to retreat first and, if forced to defend yourself, fire your weapons to disable the enemy not destroy him?"

Hidatsu nodded. "Because some of their ships might be armed with some kind of black hole technology that if damaged, might initiate a time/space wave that could spread across the galaxy. I don't pretend to understand all the physics, but I know enough to be wary about it."

"It's right that you should be," returned Jules. "I've been tasked by Military Intelligence to make sure it never happens. Some weeks ago, a Navy ship, the *John Crosse*, was stolen by parties unknown. That, in turn, sunk negotiations with the Coalition aimed at coming to an agreement to disavow use of black hole tech. News had somehow reached enemy negotiators that the ship was being used as part of a secret Terran project to develop the technology for itself even as it negotiated with the Coalition. Negotiations broke down with the result that the Coalition continues to use the technology while our own forces must stand off for fear of accidentally rupturing an enemy ship's containment unit and loosing a time/space wave that could eventually destroy the whole galaxy. Believe me, that is very likely. In any case, evidence pointed to a group of renegade scientists who stole the Navy ship and who have retreated somewhere to continue working on the black hole tech against the wishes of the Consortium. I traced one of them to Earth and then to Alpha Centauri. We lost him there but I have reason to believe he rendezvoused with the others and is hiding out at PER-734..."

"Never heard of it," said Hidatsu rubbing his chin. "It sounds like it's in the Perseus arm..."

"It is."

"Then we've got some traveling to do. It could be dangerous you know. We'll be traveling without an escort. After the attack on the yards, no colony is deemed safe now. There's going to be a general retreat to the home worlds and every ship will be needed for security."

"We have a couple things going for us, Captain," said Jules. "I believe the traitor that has been informing the enemy of our movements has been stopped, so the Coalition will have no idea of what's become of us once we leave for the Perseus arm. Also, like the Consortium, the Coalition has never been too keen about expanding across the Gulf to Perseus so we shouldn't encounter any enemy patrols."

"True. Well, no sense wasting time then. Mr. Jefferson, set course across the Gulf to Perseus. I'll confer with navigation about getting us from there to PER-734."

"Aye, sir," said the XO stalking from the room.

"If you'll excuse me, Mr. Santros...Miss Mooney," said Hidatsu, sketching a salute. "It'll be a few weeks before we can complete the crossing, and I'm sure we'll have plenty of time to talk further in the interval."

Mooney looked at Jules after they were alone.

"You have any plans in mind for when we get there?"

"Not really," Jules admitted.

"What if you guessed wrong and Heintzle and the others aren't at PER-734?"

"I don't really want to consider that."

A few days later, they were standing in the little observation deck forward looking out of the few plas-glass outlets into open space. Far ahead a thin, misty line stretched across utter blackness, the only evidence of the Perseus arm of the Milky Way far across what was popularly known as the Gulf...that multi-light year gap between the Orion and Perseus arms of the galaxy.

Behind them, as a quick glance at a rear view of the ship being displayed on several monitors showed, was the thick swarm of stars that made up the Orion arm and somewhere, tens of thousands of light years farther on, the central hub of the galaxy.

Just now, on the other side of the plas-glass enclosure, was mostly empty space. Deep blackness dotted only by a few pinpoints of light indicating other, infinitely distant galaxies, all racing in every direction away from each other. The sensation as the *Constitution* left the Orion arm was one of stepping off a cliff into empty air.

"Feels strange, doesn't it?" asked Mooney, wanting to hold Jules' arm but not daring. "Like going off the edge of the world."

"Now I know how Christopher Columbus must have felt when he first lost sight of land on his voyage to discover the new world," said Jules not taking his eyes from the enclosure.

"I wonder what we'll find over there?"

Jules shrugged, hands in the pockets of the ship's coverall uniforms they had been issued.

"Somehow, I can't wait till this is all over," said Mooney. "I want to go home."

"If there's a galaxy to go home to," Jules said, thinking aloud.

He never felt it when Mooney took his arm.

Chapter Twenty-one

Retreat

Captain Nikolai Iescu sat in his command chair watching the steady string of shuttles rising up from the otherwise barren moonscape of Callisto. Any other time he would be admiring the awesome site of Jupiter with its drifting red spot as it dominated the heavens beyond the little satellite. This visit was like no other time he ever sailed the Jovian system. This time, he was here to oversee the mass evacuation of the resort area.

Since the surprise attack on the Proxima yards two weeks before, the Consortium had been forced to go public with the news that the war with the Coalition was going badly. Through some means, and Iescu, like many in the Navy, knew it was due to the enemy's use of black hole technology, something the Consortium had no defense against as yet, the enemy took the upper hand in the contest necessitating extreme measures by the government to protect its citizens.

As a result, a general order had been issued for a retreat from non-essential or sparsely populated colonies to worlds more central to the Consortium where naval forces could be concentrated for better protection.

Barnard's Star, Altair, Epsilon 12, Rigel 2, New Calvary, as well as Alpha Centauri, and the Sol system of course, were to form the last line of defense with orders to accommodate the populations of their sister colonies such as the vacation resort here at Callisto.

Already, every space aboard the *City of Rome* had been filled up with residents, hotel workers, and other concessionaires who remained behind after the earlier departure of honeymooners and other vacationers on commercial liners requisitioned for the evacuation. Now, they were being redirected to other ships in the squadron, a half dozen cruisers and a tender. Iescu estimated that there would be enough room.

Having lingered here supervising the evacuation, he was anxious to get going, not wishing to be caught by surprise if Coalition battleships suddenly appeared out of nowhere as they had been doing. Not that he feared a fight. He had confidence in himself and his crew. It was just that this time, his ships would be filled with vulnerable civilians with orders not to shoot to kill enemy vessels.

That was no way to fight and win a war. As the battle lines shifted closer to the home worlds, the Consortium would be forced to retaliate with more vigor, taking the chance on destroying a Coalition ship and perhaps setting in motion the time/space effects of the feared black hole technology.

For his part, Iescu thought it worth the chance. Better to risk the danger than to live under the heel of a damned Drool!

Chapter Twenty-two

Confrontation

It loomed before them bigger than any planet they had ever seen and it was still a full light year away.

"Look at the size of it," murmured an awed crewman manning the navigation hut.

Jules and Mooney were standing on the bridge somewhat to the side of Hidatsu sitting in the command chair.

Though he knew what to expect, Jules, too, was impressed.

PER-734 had been discovered over fifty Earth years before but visited fewer than three times so far as he knew, and one of those times was he and Joan's fly-by some years ago while mapping the region for the Survey. They hadn't lingered because at the time it was not known what interest the Coalition might have had in the area.

"How big is it, Dr. Santros?" asked Hidatsu, who had learned over the past several weeks of Jules' standing in the scientific community.

"It's radius from the collapsed star at its core is about four billion miles," replied Jules, watching the main view screen that showed a black sphere whose shape could only be made out against the glow of the still distant Perseus Arm. "Roughly the distance of Pluto from Sol. A perfectly formed natural Dyson's sphere, maybe the only one in existence."

"You think it was the mass of the collapsed star that formed it?"

"Couldn't be anything else. It must have begun billions and billions of years ago. Maybe from when the universe was first formed. It would take that long to draw so much matter to itself. Likely, it was a proto-star, a star that was never quite able to generate the energy needed to ignite properly. Instead, it collapsed, forming a super heavy core that began drawing in nearby matter."

"Like a black hole for instance?"

"Something like that but not as powerful. Strong enough though, to attract dark matter, the microscopic stuff that permeates the entire universe, leftover material from the big bang. Obviously, it was all drawn here over billions of years, coalescing somehow around the star's event horizon where the shell began to form."

"Do you think it's safe for a ship to land on?" asked Mooney staring at the slowly growing size of the distant object that was encircled by a glowing ring of debris only visible from a certain angle.

"By now I would judge so, but I wouldn't take any kind of chance on a landing until a thorough study could be done of the gravitics surrounding the sphere," warned Jules.

"So, if they're here, the renegades likely wouldn't be on the surface?" asked Hidatsu.

"Right. My guess is they're either in orbit or located on one of the larger pieces of debris being drawn to the ring surrounding the sphere."

"Mr. Terrece," said Hidatsu to a crewman manning the sensor array, "can you read anything down there?"

"I'm not having an easy time, Captain, that's for sure," said Terrece. "A combination of electro-gravitic clutter is interfering with my instruments."

"That'll be caused by the interaction between the star's gravimetric pull and friction generated by the structure of the sphere itself. It's all held together through a delicate balance of dynamic forces."

"How delicate?" asked Hidatsu.

"Oh, don't worry. It's not like it'll just fall apart when you touch it. If this ship crashed into the sphere head on at full thrust, it's not likely to cause any more disturbance than it would doing the same thing on Earth. We're talking about massive, galactic structures here."

"Well, I'm relieved anyway."

"So, how do we proceed from here?" Jules wanted to know. "Finding the stolen ship is going to be like looking for a needle in a haystack, especially with all that interference out there."

"We don't have to look for them," said Hidatsu. "We'll let them tell us where they are. Assuming that they haven't shut down all of the ship's systems, we should be able to find them by picking up traces of routine ship operations such as power levels, life support functions, and even some hyper-waveband dormancy signals. That last is something civilians might not know anything about. Besides, without a full crew, it's likely the renegades have been too busy conducting basic operating functions to worry much about anything else."

"Sensor officer will begin monitoring all bands," ordered the XO.

"Rig for silent running," added Hidatsu. "Search pattern Sigma."

"Battle stations," called the XO.

"Battle stations?" asked Mooney. "Is that necessary?"

"I didn't rise through the ranks by being reckless, Miss Mooney," noted Hidatsu. "It's likely these scientists you're looking for are untrained in the operations of Naval vessels, but there's no sense in taking chances."

As crewmen scrambled about taking their stations, Jules and Mooney just tried to stay out of their way. Gradually, things settled down as the big ship assumed a wide orbit around the sphere and well outside the range of debris being slowly drawn to the area.

Jules' attention was taken by a surface monitor showing the curvature of the sphere as objects, picking up speed as they approached it, went on to crash below, adding their mass to the shell surrounding the dead star. He wondered just how powerful the dwarf-matter inside really was? Could it be a black hole did lurk somewhere in its interior?

As the *Constitution* continued to circle the sphere, a multi-colored glow rose over its horizon, soon revealed as a streamer of interstellar gas dotted with stars; a nebula, as it was being drawn in by the object's irresistible pull.

"Incredible," breathed Hidatsu, watching the drama unfold on the bridge's main screen.

"Sir," called the sensor officer. "We have a signal."

"Locate and identify."

"It's an HBD sir," replied the officer, then realizing their guests might not understand, "a hyper-waveband signal."

"Can you follow it in?"

"No problem, sir."

"Feed the coordinates to navigation," ordered Jefferson. "Stay on top of it."

"Any other substantiating signals?" Hidatsu wanted to know.

"Getting some low energy readings, sir," said the sensor officer, putting a finger to his earpiece. "Definitely life support."

"We've got them," said Hidatsu to Jules. "Adjust forward cameras to the HBD and follow it in."

"Aye, sir."

"Propulsion. Steady as she goes. We don't want to spook them."

"Aye, sir."

Slowly, the great ship eased its way inward from its previous orbit, the navigator demonstrating his skill as he steered between the increasingly crowded space surrounding the sphere. All around them now, debris began to pick up with some quite large chunks mixed in, then it was there, dead ahead, the *John Crosse*.

"Steady as she goes," said Hidatsu, his eyes riveted on the vessel that slowly grew as they approached it.

With more detail in view, Jules could see the ship was a cruiser, barely half the size of the *Constitution* and so bristled with fewer gun emplacements that were no less dangerous for that. Ominous looking recesses in its bow hinted at pulse cannons that could be brought into play if those aboard had the inclination.

Jules hoped they didn't and began going over his plan of what he wanted to do when the ship had finally been found. Unless the renegades offered resistance of some kind, he would ask to come over and try to talk them into surrendering. After all, their cause was pointless now that they had been discovered. He hoped to convince them of that and avoid the necessity of a boarding party and the humiliation of seizure and arrest.

"Stop engines," ordered Hidatsu.

"Stop engines," repeated the XO.

"Engines stopped," said the propulsion officer.

"Propulsion. Use thrusters as needed to maintain position," said the XO.

"Aye."

"Now comes the tricky part," said Hidatsu. "Communications, open a channel to the *John Crosse.*"

"Channel open, sir."

"This is Captain Paul Hidatsu of the Consortium ship *Constitution*," opened Hidatsu. "Identify yourselves."

There was a pause before a voice came over their earpieces.

"We are a group of Terran researchers conducting experimentation," said the voice. "What is your business here? We did not request any aid."

"Heintzle," whispered Jules.

"You misunderstand," said Hidatsu, playing along for the moment. "We're not here to answer any distress calls, we're here to arrest you in the name of the Consortium."

Silence again then, "I'm afraid there's been some mistake, Captain..."

"No mistake," said Hidatsu firmly. "Our sensors identify your vessel as the *John Crosse,* a Navy vessel that was reported stolen from the Sol system months ago. As such, I have orders to impound it and to apprehend and return anyone aboard for questioning and possible prosecution."

"If those aboard refuse to cooperate?"

"We will board the ship and fulfill our orders," replied Hidatsu. "But know if such an extreme contingency is forced upon us, it will not go well for you when you're returned to Sol."

Jules thought he heard some chuckling from the other ship.

"I doubt things will go well for us in any case, Captain. Tell me, is Dr. Jules Santros with you by any chance?"

Hidatsu saw no reason not to admit it. "He is."

"Hello, Jules," said the voice. "You are nothing if not persistent. A quality, as I recall, that endeared you to our superiors in Military Intelligence."

"Hello, Georg," returned Jules. "I might say the same of you seeing as how you've refused to drop that research we were working on."

"It had too great a potential, Jules. Our superiors were thinking too small. They had too limited imaginations. Shutting down the project was premature...especially considering the problems the Consortium is having with the Coalition these days."

"A problem exacerbated by you and your colleagues," countered Jules. "If you hadn't acted as rashly as you did, both sides would have come to an agreement on use of the technology and thousands of lives saved."

"I regret that, but often in order for science to advance, there must be casualties."

It was Jules' turn to remain silent then.

"By your silence I assume you disagree, Jules," continued Heintzle. "What say we call a temporary truce with the good captain's permission and you can come over for a little chat? Perhaps this situation can be defused without the need for boarding parties, arrests and such."

With a signal from Hidatsu to put Heintzle on hold, the captain turned to Jules.

"Seems like you and he are reading from the same script, Doctor. What do you think? Is there any reason not to proceed as you planned?"

Jules gave it some thought before replying.

"I think so," he said. "Heintzle and the rest of them are reasonable men. They're not insane despite the lengths they've gone to in this quixotic enterprise. There's still a chance I can reason with them."

Hidatsu sighed. "My orders are to do what you ask. Open channel." He nodded to Jules.

"Georg," said Jules. "Stand by. I'm coming over."

"Excellent"

"Jules, are you sure you ought to do this?" asked Mooney. "What if you're wrong about them and they take you hostage or something?"

"My orders are to stop them," reminded Hidatsu. "Any way I have to."

"I stand by our plan..."

"Your plan, you mean..." said Mooney, clearly more concerned than a professional colleague should be.

"There's no other choice," insisted Jules, uncomfortably. "It's either me going over to convince them to surrender or use force. Who knows what might happen if they've managed to create their own black hole over there."

"I still don't like it but...be careful," said Mooney, giving him a quick, little hug.

"I will," reassured Jules, fighting to keep from feeling anything more about Mooney than professional concern.

Chapter Twenty-three

Collapse

The trip by shuttle from the *Constitution* to the *John Crosse* was relatively swift and uneventful with Jules being cycled through the airlock mechanism with little formality. On the other side, he was greeted by his former colleagues with Georg in the lead.

"Good to see you again, Jules," Georg was saying, his hand extended.

Hesitating for only a moment, Jules took it. "I wish it were in better circumstances."

Georg waved aside such concerns. "I won't insult your intelligence by saying something like not bothering yourself with it, but I do wish you'd keep an open mind as we explain our motives."

"It won't be easy considering the number of times you tried to kill me," replied Jules.

"I'm sorry about that," said Heintzle with some contrition. "Once you've heard us out, I'm sure you'll at least understand our desperation to keep from being interfered with."

"It would have been even harder if I'd been killed," pointed out Jules, not unreasonably.

"Well, be that as it may, you're here now. Will you hear us out?"

"I know all of you were opposed to shutting down research in black hole technology when the decision was made," said Jules. "I assume none of you wanted to leave it at that."

"Something like that," conceded Heintzle.

"We did it for science," declared Henry Martine, a heavy atom expert and not surprisingly, supervisor of the nitinol project.

"The military had no right to shut us down," added the team's

145

quantum mech theorist, Klaus Saltoumas. "We have a duty as scientists to pursue knowledge wherever it leads."

"Even if it leads to the destruction of the galaxy?" countered Jules.

"It was for that very reason that we needed to continue," replied Saltoumas. "How else could we learn how to tame the technology?"

"All it would take was a single lab accident, one miscalculation, even a lone madman if you will, to set those forces loose," said Jules. "I know what I'm talking about. I had to deal with such an accident first hand when I came across a disabled Coalition warship that had used black hole tech."

"But that's just it," said Martine. "We've solved the problem of security, or at least we believe we're almost there."

"Gentlemen," said Heintzle, "why don't we hold off on this discussion until we show Jules the progress we've made. Then we can talk about it on a more fully informed level."

So saying, Heintzle gestured for Jules to follow him.

As they moved along, the gravitic engineer filled in the awkward silence with some explanatory talk.

"I'm sorry we caused the trouble we did when we took control of this ship," said Heintzle. "As you know, the only way anyone can get around Consortium space is either by naval vessel or commercial liner. Any lesser form of transportation would have been inadequate."

"By doing so, you wrecked negotiations with the Coalition," pointed out Jules. "Or didn't you take that into account? Perhaps maybe you did?"

"It had crossed our minds," admitted Heintzle. "If it did, so much the better as it would force the Consortium to continue research into artificial black hole technology. Unfortunately, that failed to happen and we were forced to proceed with our plans."

"Which was...what? Set up your own lab somewhere?"

"Exactly. Something I suspect you realized quite early on."

"You needed the ship for more than just transportation. The logical answer was that you needed a sophisticated platform that could be moved as needed while allowing you to work undisturbed. By the way, how did you manage stealing the ship in the first place? One doesn't go around hijacking a Navy cruiser at the drop of a hat."

"Well, we had help..."

"Bentley O'Shea?"

"You know of him?"

"Unless I miss my guess, he's now the guest of your former boss, director Leclerc."

"Ah. I guess it'll do no harm admitting O'Shea did help us to acquire the ship. Of course, Ivar here had no little role in the scheme as well."

Jules looked over to the cyber specialist, who nodded.

"You see, O'Shea and I met at a diplomatic function a couple years ago," continued Heintzle. "He was in the company of a charming young psychologist..."

"Don't tell me," said Jules. "Marta Sandoz."

"You have done well on this case, Jules."

"Too well, I sometimes think. Sandoz was found dead after an attempt on my life early in the investigation."

"Do tell. She was quite a charming girl."

"I suppose she was the one who passed the information about the stolen ship to the Coalition delegation during the negotiations?"

"I assume so," said Heintzle. "I'm not sure as O'Shea never told me he intended to use the theft to undermine the negotiations."

"I suppose you also didn't know about the Coalition attack at Proxima that was intended to kill me either?"

"I hadn't heard about that," said Heintzle, and Jules believed him. "Sorry."

"Don't be, because it was you that set that trap on Earth that came much closer to killing me than the Coalition Navy did."

"Again. Sorry about that. That trap was meant for anyone coming to look for me..."

"Was that why you used the black hole tech project cover name in your records? Only someone who was part of the project would have picked up on that clue."

"Well, you have me there, Jules," admitted Heintzle. "Of course, I didn't know who Leclerc would be sending after us, but you were always a possibility, of course."

"So, you took the *John Crosse* out here," said Jules, changing the subject.

"We figured it was far enough away and well outside either the Coalition or Consortium's areas of interest. Did you know Aeroflotilla Laboratories sponsored an expedition out here some years ago? They did. That was before my services were loaned out to Military Intelligence. I was on that mission and remembered the area when it came time to decide where we were to conduct our research. The unique gravitic effects of PER-734 would not only provide some measure of cover from long range sensors but afford an interesting environment for testing."

"Too bad you weren't as familiar with naval operations and capabilities as you were with PER-734."

"Good point," admitted Heintzle. "But water under the bridge as they used to say. Ah. Here we are."

They had come to the engine compartment and following Heintzle inside, Jules was once more confronted by the awful and wondrous sight of a temporal black hole, its unfathomable power somehow harnessed, likely within the tenuous confines of a radical cube. The whole arrangement was connected in to the ship's sub-photon engines, obviously with the intention of using the black hole's power in the same manner as the Coalition was doing. Something moved deep in the pit of his stomach as he contemplated the incredible danger represented by what he was seeing.

"Recognize it?" asked Heintzle, smiling.

"A temporal black hole," replied Jules, not taking his eyes from the glare of the singularity.

"Yes, we built it based on our research with Military Intelligence. Producing a hydrostatic core, we heated it to two thousand K allowing for the ionization of hydrogen and helium atoms. That permitted excess energies to escape in the form of Hawking radiation. Collapse followed and..."

"A star is born."

"Cute. From there, it was a simple matter of induced starvation of stellar nucleosynthesis forcing the creation of a white-dwarf and thence, a black hole..."

"Nothing we didn't accomplish in the laboratory before. The real question is containment. We always had a problem maintaining its integrity. The radical cube used as a containment unit and existing as it does in four dimensions was a successful alternative in keeping the singularity stable in space, but time always remained a problem."

"And it remains so," interjected Martine.

"Henry..."

"You know it's so, Georg," said Martine. "Even though we had your report from Cygnus Alpha 12 including the news the Coalition scientists built the radical cube first before growing a black hole inside it, we still haven't been able to lick the containment problem."

"You're too pessimistic, Henry..."

"The cube is unstable, Georg, and so long as it is, this continued research is not only useless but dangerous. In fact, our being located here within the flux of PER-734 has made the containment unit even more unstable. The entire sphere is surrounded by an electro-magnetic charge that interferes with the cube's theoretical foundations."

"Nonsense," insisted Heintzle, moving toward the unseen containment unit where its multiple angles and planes existed more in theory than reality, holding in suspension an artificial hole in space/time.

"Georg, don't..." pleaded Martine as the rest of the group leaned forward as if actually being drawn in by the harnessed power of the black hole.

"We need to prove to Jules our work has shown progress, true progress, if we are to convince him to advise the government to let us continue with our research," said Heintzle. "Or have you forgotten there is a Consortium battleship outside with its guns aimed directly at us?"

"There's no need to take chances like...Georg, stop."

It was too late. Desperate to save the situation, Heintzle pulled a pulse-pistol from beneath his lab coverall and aimed it at the unseen cube. As Jules stood, taken by surprise, Martine lunged toward his colleague.

Although he managed to strike up Heintzle's gun hand, it was not enough. The weapon went off and a high-pressure pulse leaped from the weapon and hit the screen with a force that sent streaks of energy, visible as charges of electricity, coursing along the pressure lines that made up the radical cube.

For a minute, as everyone held their collective breaths, there was every sign that the unit maintained its integrity. Suddenly, light flickered along its hidden seams, revealing fault lines and exposing all space/time to the effects of the singularity.

Horrified, Jules could only recall the close call he experienced on Cygnus Alpha 12 and how nearly the whole galaxy came to extinction. With a prayer on his lips and thoughts of Joan back on Mars as well as Mooney on the *Constitution*, both blissfully unaware of the danger threatening them and everyone else they had ever known, he prepared to once again leap to the rescue, hoping he could repair the damage in the same way he did before, by rebuilding the radical cube from the inside out.

Before he could take two steps toward the breached containment unit, Martine stopped him.

"Head back to your ship, Jules," he shouted. "I'll attempt the shutdown. Don't worry, I read your report thoroughly and understand how you managed the containment. The conclusions reached by our superiors was correct. This technology is too dangerous to use. Even if we managed to find a way to contain it, the chance would still remain that either something could go wrong or that human fallibility would tell. Go back. Get away while you can."

With that, Martine plunged into the singularity's expanding event horizon and once again, Jules noted the distortion effect that made it appear that Martine was at once standing still while also slowly being pulled into the space/time vortex.

Around him, the others talked excitedly. Some moved to work stations to monitor Martine's progress while others still held an astonished Heintzle from plunging himself into the event horizon.

Determined to do what he could, Jules moved to take hold of Martine's waist to anchor him in the present even as his arms and face stretched as they would in a funhouse mirror. Then, as if in slow motion, he saw or sensed, the continued breakdown of the containment unit. Martine, for some reason, was not taking the approach Jules had back on Cygnus Alpha 12. He was doing something else...

Chapter Twenty-three

Rewind

"Sir," called the sensor officer. "We have a signal."

"Locate and identify!"

"It's an HBD sir," replied the officer. "A hyper-waveband signal."

"Can you follow it in?"

"No problem, sir."

"Feed the coordinates to navigation," ordered Jefferson. "Stay on top of it."

"Any other substantiating signals?" Hidatsu wanted to know.

"Getting some low energy readings, sir," said the sensor officer, putting a finger to his earpiece. "Definitely life support."

"We've got them," said Hidatsu to Jules. "Adjust forward cameras to the HBD and follow it in."

"Aye, sir."

"Propulsion. Steady as she goes. We don't want to spook them."

"Aye, sir."

Slowly, the great ship eased its way inward from its previous orbit. Then it was there, dead ahead, the *John Crosse*.

"Steady as she goes," said Hidatsu as the *Constitution* approached.

With more detail in view, Jules could see the other ship was a cruiser, barely half the size of the *Constitution* with correspondingly fewer gun emplacements. Ominous looking recesses in its bow hinted at pulse cannons that could be brought into play if those aboard had the inclination.

"Sir," said the sensor officer. "I have some funny readings here."

"Explain."

"Not sure, sir, but they appear to be similar to the gravitics we use for our artificial gravity..."

"You're sure you're not picking up the flux from the sphere?" asked Jules. "Remember, there could be a black hole in there. A collapsed star at the very least..."

"Could be, sir, but...wait one...it's spiking, sir."

"Let me see what you've got there." Jules studied the various instruments until his forehead creased in puzzlement. "That's funny. There's been a huge jump in gravitational waves."

"So? Is that important?" asked Mooney.

"It would be if there was any evidence of a massive stellar event, but there isn't one. Otherwise, I don't see how it could be possible..." Then it hit him. Hawking radiation was released when quantum effects occurred at the interface between a black hole and its event horizon. A shell had formed on the horizon. The only way there could be a jump in gravitational waves was if something destabilized the balance between the Hawking energy emitted by the event horizon and the amount of mass being consumed by the black hole inside the shell. The resulting gravitational waves would cause a rip in space and time.

Suddenly, as mysteriously as they appeared, the gravitational waves were gone.

Jules thought hard for a few seconds, but it didn't take long for him to reason out the explanation. It wasn't good.

"Captain," he cried suddenly, "turn the ship about right now. Engage sub-photon drive immediately. We need to be a million miles away from here as soon as possible."

Hidatsu, keyed by the excitement in Jules' voice, asked no questions but ordered engagement of the ship's engines. In minutes, minutes to Jules felt more like hours, the sub-photon drive fired up and taken the *Constitution* far out of the vicinity of PER-734.

"Now, will you explain—" Hidatsu was saying before Jules cut him off.

"What are your instruments showing now?" he asked the sensor officer.

"Still more of those gravitics, sir. They're definitely coming from the *John Crosse*."

"What does...?" Hidatsu was asking when suddenly the view on the forward monitor, sent by previously deployed remote cameras, showed the *John Crosse* as it collapsed in on itself. In seconds, a ship that was able to hold a crew of fifty was reduced to a mass of crumpled metal the size of a basketball.

"My God," Jules mumbled, awed at the sight.

"What? What's happened?" asked Mooney, taking hold of Jules' arm.

In another few seconds, the ball of metal compressed even further. There was no evidence at all it had once been a man-made object. It began to lose its position over the gigantic sphere below, its orbit deteriorating quickly. In seconds, it fell thousands of miles, toward the sphere's surface, picking up speed quickly until suddenly, it disappeared from view, crashing through that ancient billion, billion-year-old crust, hurtling to join the invisible speck of super heavy mass at its heart.

The violence of the collision between the crumpled ship and the crust had taken its toll. Cracks began to form in its surface as heat generated by the Hawking energy that was suddenly released quickly increased, devouring the shell and causing it to collapse toward the dwarf matter at its heart.

Immediately, the *Constitution*'s instruments began to go haywire in a storm of gravitational waves that lashed the ship as time was speeded up and slowed down and the very shape of space was bent and twisted.

As it was, the ship's tintinabulum hull emerged from the storm deformed but intact. As instruments came back on line and departments reported to the bridge, it was discovered that little else had changed.

"That's what I call a close call," said Jules, sighing in relief.

"What the hell just happened?" demanded Hidatsu, still a little disoriented after the experience.

"The sudden collapse of the shell upset the balance between the dwarf matter inside and the event horizon," explained Jules. "The violence of that sudden shift in the status quo triggered the release of gravitational waves. If we hadn't escaped in time, the ship would have been torn apart as space all around us shifted and what was left drawn into the resulting gravity well."

"So, were we too late?" asked Hidatsu. "Did the renegades'

experimenting do them in?"

"Yes," was all Jules could say. "Too late."

"So, what happened to the *John Crosse*?" asked Mooney.

"I can only speculate, but my guess is that something went wrong with their project," said Jules, still staring at the forward monitor that now showed only empty space where the *John Crosse* had been minutes before. "For the ship to have collapsed like that, the containment unit must have failed. That was the problem we had in our earlier research. We could never lick the fourth dimensional factor. That was always the weak point...that and the inherently unstable nature of a radical cube."

"I still don't get much of what you're saying, Doctor."

"Simply put, the containment unit must have collapsed, unleashing the unlimited power of the artificial black hole that drew in everything around it including anybody aboard that ship."

"How awful," gasped Mooney.

"It was quick anyway," said Jules. "I'm sure no one aboard had a chance to know what was happening. Anyway, once the thing collapsed, its own gravitic force would have drawn it toward the flux field being generated by the black hole inside the sphere. Only something with a pull that powerful could have overcome the one generated by the artificial black hole. Anyway, that accounts for why the artificial one was drawn downward. By now, the two have been fused into a single super-singularity. That fusion and the collapse of the shell would have been enough to unleash the storm of gravitational waves that followed."

"How were you able to warn us in time to get the ship out of there?" Hidatsu wanted to know.

"Gravitational waves only occur following stellar events of massive proportions. Since nothing of the kind happened yet, I reasoned the waves we were detecting were coming from the future...in effect, warning us of a catastrophe to come. The only thing that could have been was the collapse of the shell."

"The waves were coming from the future?"

"As I mentioned, gravitational waves have the ability to shift time and space," said Jules.

"So, you're saying this gravitational wave storm that happened in the future shifted back a few minutes in time where our instruments picked them up?"

"That's right. Providential wasn't it?"

Hidatsu took off his cap and wiped his forehead with his sleeve. "I'll say."

There was quiet a moment as everyone took in all that happened.

"Navigator," said Hidatsu at last. "Plot us a course away from here. I don't want to take any chance of being caught by any super-black hole. Not now."

"Aye, sir," replied the navigator, not without some nervousness at the possible danger.

"Is there something bothering you, Jules?" asked Mooney. "Something you're not telling us?"

"Not really. Just thinking about the time I ended up in the same situation those poor devils down there did and what I had to do to get out of it."

"So?"

"Well, I was wondering if Georg or anyone else aboard the *John Crosse* was able to do the same."

"Judging from what we just saw, I doubt it."

"Not necessarily. If someone was able to do what I did, we'd never know about it."

Hidatsu noticed the little frown that creased Mooney's forehead as though she wondered what Jules meant, but before she could pursue the subject further, his attention was diverted by a message coming in over his personal earphone.

"Who is this?" he asked, placing a finger to his ear.

"I can't say just now, Captain," said the voice. "But if you'll come to your cabin, I can explain. We need to talk. Be sure you come alone."

"If this is some kind of joke, you're going to be one damn sorry crewman whoever you are."

Hidatsu rose from his command chair and approached the XO.

"Jefferson," he said in a lowered voice, "you have the conn."

"Aye, sir."

"I'm going to my cabin. If I don't call in ten minutes, send a couple men down to find me."

"Aye, sir," replied the XO, not inquiring further.

Hidatsu headed for the exit, leaving Jules and Mooney to continue their conversation. With rising anger at whoever it was that had clearly invaded his cabin, he charged down the corridor leading to officer country, making sure the safety on his pulse-pistol was released.

Not bothering to signal his arrival, he ordered the computer to open the door to his cabin and stepped inside. There, to his surprise, stood Jules.

"What...? How did you...?"

"Prepare yourself for the unbelievable, captain," said Jules. "You won't need that pistol."

Overcoming his surprise, Hidatsu holstered the weapon.

"Now what's the idea, Doctor?"

"Well, for one thing, I'm not the Jules you just left on the bridge."

"What do you mean?"

"I mean that I'm Jules from a timeline that's been erased. One that you now know nothing about."

"I still don't understand..."

"Here it is in a nutshell. In another timeline, the *Constitution* arrived here at PER-734 just as you remember, but in that instance, we arrived in time to contact the renegades before their project failed. I went over alone to talk to them and while I was there, Georg, in an attempt to prove to me that the radical cube containing the artificial black hole they'd constructed was safe, fired at it with a pulse-pistol. Unfortunately, the structure wasn't as strong as he believed. There was a breach and the black hole's energy was released. In minutes, the ship around us was going to collapse in on itself. At the last minute, another of my former colleagues, a Dr. Henry Martine, attempted to control the collapse using the same method I did at Alpha Cygnus 12."

Jules paused to heave a sigh.

"Beyond that, I don't know. But considering I find myself here, aboard the *Constitution* again, I can only conclude that Martine managed to save me by sending me back in time to the point just before the collapse of their black hole. I watched it happen from the monitor here in your cabin. Just don't ask me to explain how the thing collapsed in this new timeline without me having to go over and inspiring Geo rg to take that shot...it's all wrapped up in the paradoxical laws governing temporal black holes. Anyway, I found myself in the ship's engine spaces, the same area I was when things started to go wrong aboard the *John Crosse*. After I began to realize what must have happened, I came here as the only place that I might be able to stay out of sight until I could talk to you."

"You expect me to believe all that?" asked Hidatsu wonderingly.

"Why should I lie to you?"

Hidatsu had no answer for that. Instead, he used his earphone to contact the bridge.

"Jefferson."

"Sir."

"One question. Is Dr. Santros still on the bridge?"

"Yes, sir. He and Miss Mooney are still here."

"Thanks," Hidatsu replied then, "I don't believe it."

"It's not that easy for me to believe either, Captain. What I figure is that when this same thing happened to me on Alpha Cignus 12, I re-set time, allowing everything to go back to the way it was before. Not time travel strictly speaking. What Martine must have done was quite different. In his haste, perhaps, he simply sent me back in time while making sure he and the other renegades didn't, thus ensuring that their project would not be repeated."

"So...now there are two of you?"

"I'm afraid so. What I want is to stay out of his sight...in fact, I don't want the other Jules to even know I exist. Because we're not two different people, we're exactly the same person. No difference. I know exactly how he feels, the way he thinks. When it comes time to leave the ship, I know what he's going to do. So, if you don't mind, Captain, I'd like to stay in here, out of sight, until you drop him off back at Alpha Centauri."

"And Miss Mooney...?"

"Don't tell her a thing."

It was not easy for Jules to remain confined for several weeks as the *Constitution* made its way back across the gulf to the Orion arm, even with the captain's cabin for quarters. Worse still, was being alone with his thoughts as the sacrifice he was determined to make bore down on him in all its growing significance.

At last, however, the battleship arrived in orbit above Proxima 5. By that time, Mooney had long since become reconciled to the fact Jules was committed to his wife and he could make no place for her in his heart. It was for the best however, because over the months they had worked together, she'd grown fond of him and to have undermined his loyalty to Joan would have been a betrayal of their friendship.

That, however, did not make their parting any the less easy.

"It's my understanding that both sides are headed back to the negotiating table," she was saying as she and Jules walked to the shuttle that would take him down to the Proxima rocket field.

"Well, once the Consortium was able to present them with O'Shea as well as the evidence we sent by hyper-waveband of how the threat posed by the renegades had ended, the Coalition had to admit that the Consortium never had any intentions of pursuing black hole tech at their expense," said Jules. "More to the point, the visuals of the *John Crosse* collapsing on itself were damned powerful. They had to have shaken up even those Zhapoologani hard cases about the danger they were placing themselves in."

"But the war will go on."

"It will."

Conversation seemed to dry up then. There was not much to say. Jules made his decision to return home and Mooney was to go on to the ministry.

At the door of the shuttle, Jules extended his hand.

"Well, Miss Mooney...Manda...it was good working with you. I admit, at first, I wasn't crazy about having you tag along, but it was good to have someone else to bounce ideas off of."

"Not to mention watching your back a time or two," said Mooney, ignoring his hand and throwing her arms around his neck. "I'll miss you, Jules."

Not unresponsive, Jules hugged her back.

"I'll miss you too, Manda. You know," he said, holding her at arm's length, "in any other lifetime..."

"Don't say it," begged Mooney. "We've been through all that

already. Better let it be."

"You're right," smiled Jules. "Goodbye."

"Bye," said Mooney, watching as he passed into the shuttle and disappeared toward the passenger area.

Back in the ready room, Mooney watched a monitor showing the bay doors opening and the shuttle slowly rise, clearing the hull of the *Constitution* to bask in the light from Alpha Centauri's suns.

In another minute, it was almost gone from sight, boosted by its thrusters.

A lump in her throat, Mooney fought to keep from tearing up.

"Manda," said a familiar voice behind her.

Startled, Mooney turned to see Jules standing inside the hatch to the ready room.

"Jules? How...?" Instinctively, Mooney turned back to the monitor that showed the last of the shuttle as it vanished from sight.

Jules walked over and switched off the monitor.

"Jules, how could...?"

"Manda, I want you to listen for a minute," said Jules, and he proceeded to give her the same explanation of the events that took place at PER-734 as he had told them to Captain Hidatsu.

"You mean, all this time you've been hiding in the captain's cabin?" asked an incredulous Mooney.

"It wasn't fun, believe me. I couldn't take the chance of the other Jules getting wind of me. You understand, don't you?"

"I think so. But don't worry. I'm not holding it against you...does that matter to you?"

"I think it does," admitted Jules. "You've made it pretty hard for me to keep from falling in love with you, you know. In any other lifetime..."

Mooney laughed.

"What's so funny?"

"You are. The other Jules just said the exact same thing."

"Well, we are the same person, after all. I mean, exactly the same. He's not somebody else. He's me. He's the man, dare I say it, you fell in love with."

"You can dare..."

Jules moved toward Mooney, falling into her arms.

"It's not going to be easy, Manda," he said. "I'm still the same Jules you've known all along. I still love Joan. I still want to be with her as badly as I did before. The thing is, I know I can't now. I'll always live with the nagging doubt I let the other Jules have her so I could have you..."

"No. Don't think of it like that. Like you said, the other Jules is really you too. You couldn't both have her. The only difference was that you had the upper hand. You knew that time had been altered. He didn't. You were fundamentally changed because of that knowledge. He wasn't. He was the most fitted to go back to Joan."

"I want to believe that," said Jules, looking into Mooney's eyes. "But it's not an easy thing to let another man live the only life I've ever known."

"Then we'll make you a new life," Mooney vowed.

"I'd like that," said a sober Jules. "It'll take time to sort out my emotions. To get Joan out of my system..."

"I'll wait," promised Mooney. "And so will Callisto."

Appendix

The following short story, "Swimmers in the Sea of Time," was the basis for *Extra Galactic*. Although it isn't necessary to read it first in order to understand the events of the novel, it does give a more detailed description about how Jules discovers the Coalition's use of black hole technology that in turn, provides the back story for *Extra Galaxia*. I considered briefly using it as the opening chapters of the novel but decided finally, that it would only have prevented the reader from jumping quickly into the story. That said, I felt that "Swimmers" was useful in giving those interested a more complete picture of events only briefly referred to in chapter two by Jules in his meeting with MI director Leclerc.

Swimmers in the Sea of Time

Finlay Gower fingered the key-pad in front of him and brought the *E.R. Burroughs* about, easing it into the gravity well surrounding the planet below him, whipping the spacecraft into a high orbit that would take it over most of the planet's northern hemisphere.

"Not too shabby," said his wife from her position at the navigator's console. "I barely felt it when you jinked the ship into orbit."

"Thanks, Pris," said Finlay, giving a final command to the computer, "your calculations were right on the money."

"Oh, come on, are we going to have to listen to all this mutual admiration the whole mission?"

Finlay and Pris turned together in time to see Jules Santros step fully into the pilot's cabin, with a big grin on his face.

"I see someone's glad to be here," observed Pris.

"Not just one," said Jules, "Joan's already getting our gear together." He moved up until he was standing between husband and wife, trying to see the planet's surface from the limited-area view port over the control console. "Have you tried to locate the site yet?"

"Not wasting any time, are you?" said Pris. "I haven't gotten to that yet, but if it'll make you happy..." She leaned forward and enabled the look-down sensor array that bristled on the underside of the spacecraft. Immediately, a variety of data leapt to screens spread out around her. A greenish glow suffused the cabin as computer enhanced grids, graphs and sine-waves registered their information. Under the woman's practiced eye, the confusing jumble of information came together and made sense. "We've covered most of this hemisphere on the way in; the sensors have something, but it's ill defined. As if something's distorting the readings."

"I'd say a planet whose surface is completely submerged in liquid methane would tend to be difficult to read," said Finlay.

"That shouldn't matter too much," Jules replied, not taking his eyes from the readings, "after all, the sensors aboard the *Saint John of the Cross* found the site pretty easy, and that was only a Naval cruiser."

"Don't kid yourself," said Pris. "Those military ships have sensor gear that'd put these survey vessels to shame. The Consortium gives them all the best."

"Just the same, how about it?" asked Jules.

"Well, it's here anyway. Maybe we won't be able to identify it clearly, but we should be able to zero in on its general area as an anomaly against the remainder of the surface." She sighed. "I'll need to map the whole area and have the computers study it all. It'll take a few hours."

Jules sighed. "Okay. Let us know when you've got something. I'll be with Joan in the hanger."

Jules exited the cabin and began making his way to the rear of the ship. He'd been with the Interplanetary Geological Survey for over five years, since the war began winding down, spending most of that time with his wife cataloging near-Earth worlds prior to terra-forming operations. Before that, he put in time with Military Intelligence, Science Division, retro-engineering alien tech. It was challenging work but he'd finally had his fill and was ready for some pure research maybe with some travel attached to it. He'd got that when the most active phase of the war ended and he had a chance to team up with Joan, a xeno-geologist working for the Survey. With little call for pure physics, he mostly ended up playing engineer aboard ship when he wasn't providing muscle for Joan when off it. It wasn't the most glamorous of jobs, but it was something the Terran Consortium wanted done and it got them out of the solar system. This time however, was different. It was their first inter-stellar assignment, and he intended to make the most of it.

Joan was still lugging heavy seeming equipment from the storeroom into the shuttle that sat in the center of the hangar. Her efforts made easier in the lighter gravity of the ship. Jules waited until she disappeared inside the shuttle before he dashed over and slipped in behind her.

"Jules!" she giggled, dropping the diving gear she held in her arms.

"How'd you know it was me?"

"Because Finlay wouldn't dare do something like that."

"Like what? Kiss the back of your neck?"

"No, squeezing my..."

"Hey if you're going to make such a big deal of it, forget the whole thing," said Jules in mock seriousness, gathering her into his arms and pressing his lips to hers. When he was much younger, he used to resent the Consortium's policy of allowing only single sex or married couples on interstellar flights. To avoid certain anarchic incidents similar to those that had plagued early forays in long distance space travel they said. Now, with Joan's warm body pressed to his, he couldn't imagine a more pleasant idea for long geological expeditions.

At last, they pulled themselves apart long enough for Joan to ask, "Has Pris found the site?"

"Not yet, but she'll let us know soon." Jules saw the look of impatience on his spouse' face and cast a hurried question. "Is all the gear set?"

"I was just getting the last of the oxygen recycling units aboard. All that's left is an itemized check."

"No, I think there'll be one more thing we have to do before casting off..."

~ * ~

"All systems are green," said Pris' voice from the speaker.

"Initiating green sequence...now," said Jules as he rather heavy handedly entered the command in his key-pad. Immediately, the on-board computer commenced a systems check that was completed before Jules' fingers could return to his lap. "All systems are green," he said.

"Acknowledged," said Pris. "We're making our final approach now, you two. Time minus eleven minutes and counting."

"Got it." Jules ordered the computer to open the hangar doors and in seconds felt the soft vibrations through the shuttle's deck that told him deep space was opening up directly beneath him.

"Time minus two minutes and counting."

"Line of approach is perfect," said Finlay.

"Time minus ten seconds and counting," said Pris at last. Jules began counting with her. "Eight, seven, six, five, four, three, two, one. Disengaged."

Only the instruments on his control console told Jules the shuttle had been released from the parent ship and was in an orbit of its own that would take it into the preplanned flight path to the surface of the planet.

"Have they assigned a name to this planet yet?" asked Joan from where she was strapped in behind him.

"No, it's still just a number. Hold on."

In another few seconds, the shuttle was gliding only a few hundred feet from the surface of the planet, the greenish waves of the methane ocean moving desultorily in the minuscule atmosphere and low, low temps of somewhere around minus two hundred- and ninety-degrees F. They were down and being thrown forward in the terrific shock of the contact.

"Are you okay, honey?" asked Jules, with no little concern. He never got used to the rough landings.

"No problem," was the reply, as Joan busily undid her straps.

"Don't get up yet. Let me set the stabilizers first." Jules flicked a switch that activated a separate bank of computers that would continually collect data on the planet's gravitic forces and adjust the shuttle's equilibrium on the surface of the ocean to keep it steady, an absolute necessity when its occupants would be three miles below the surface of that ocean.

"Are we positioned correctly?" asked Joan again, going through a series of calisthenic exercises to limber up before the dive.

"Right on top of it. And so far, no sign of life."

"That's good."

She had begun to empty out the equipment lockers, leaving Jules nothing to do but stare in admiration. Since the planet had no atmosphere to speak of, the one real danger of diving through the liquid methane was eliminated. If there had been any oxygen in the atmosphere at all, one spark could have turned the entire world into a miniature sun. Otherwise, no special difficulty was expected.

They stripped and took turns in the microwave shower that eliminated any bacteriological remains on their bodies that might have reacted negatively to anything native to the planet. It was a tricky business to put on the inner suits in the close confines of the shower, but it could be done in minutes. While Jules showered, Joan donned her outer suit that was more like an EVA harness than ordinary diving gear and clipped on her utility belt holding their equipment and portable data hook-up with the shuttle's computer. The planet's lighter gravity would make moving about outside almost like swimming back on Earth. When Jules had caught up to her, he pulled out the two pulse blasters they would carry with them and checked the charges. He handed one to his wife and clipped the other to his harness.

"Are we set?" he asked.

"Let's go."

Together, they moved to the airlock and sealed themselves in. Before triggering the exit code, they double checked their re-breathing apparatus and throat microphones. "Can you hear me?"

"I wonder what it's like to make love under three miles of liquid methane?" said Jules in response. "Do you think..." but he didn't finish the thought. He heard the definitive click that told him she had turned off her receiver. He winked at her through his helmet's big visor. In response, she triggered the exit code and immediately they were sinking slowly toward the surface of the greenish liquid at the bottom of the air-lock tube.

In minutes, they were surrounded by the greenish haze of the sea with the broad underside of the shuttle blocking out the weak light from the planet's sun. Together, they moved to the forward end of the shuttle and manually opened a sliding panel beneath the nose that revealed a small cage-like device. Jules tugged on the cage and felt its hidden mechanism come to life.

There was a man-sized door in its side, and when it came down even with the two of them, he opened it and waved Joan inside. After following her in, he hit a green foot switch that allowed the cage's powered descent to the ocean's floor.

An hour's uneventful ride later, the couple emerged a few hundred feet from the sea floor, the powerful set of lights mounted on the top of the cage were just enough to illuminate vague formations looming further below.

"How far off the mark are we?" asked Jules, pushing himself toward the bottom.

Joan consulted the computer. "If we aren't right on top of it, we're mighty close. All the computer can tell me is that it's having a hard time scanning the area."

Jules nodded inside his helmet. "Have any idea what we're looking for?" The question was a variation of one he'd been asking her since the *E.R. Burroughs* left Titan Station over six months before.

"No more than I did yesterday," Joan replied.

"What exactly does the Survey expect a xeno-geological team to find out here, a radioactive volcano?"

"All we know is what the data from the *'Cross* told us, and that was made in haste."

"Yeah, I know, it was limping back from action around Procyon, the Outer Arm Coalition tried to move in on some of our colonies out there."

"Right. At first, the military thought it might have been a downed ship or something, but the readings were all wrong, not regular enough. So, the whole thing was bumped down the ladder until it got to us."

"Well, whatever gets us out of the Sol system is okay by me," said Jules. "If it *is* geological, you must have some ideas about it."

"I did until a few minutes ago, but looking over these readings now, I'm being forced to go back to square one."

"What kind of readings?" Jules used a hand thruster to drift closer to Joan to look over her shoulder at the data link on her cuff.

Joan shook her head. "Mostly the ship's sensors just can't penetrate the anomaly area. They can't even give us accurate global mapping data."

"You mean we're swimming blind?" Jules hadn't meant for the remark to sound like a joke.

"That's exactly it."

"What about life signs?"

"Right now, I can't get anything out of this thing, but according to our generalized readings before coming down, the sea holds only microbial life forms."

Jules grunted and said, "You're the boss down here. What do you want to do?"

"Are you kidding?" Joan punched off the data link and dove forward.

They continued to move about for another hour or so until, in the glare of their chest beams, the ocean bottom began to appear from the murk. Presently, the outlines of strange geological formations resolved themselves in the reaching light. They were high, conical, bee-hive like structures that, as they continued to move downward, reached up all around them, most with their crowns collapsed from the incessant erosion of millions of years of being the victims of corrosive methanol.

"What do you make of these?" asked Jules, peering down into the pitchy blackness of an open cone.

"Tectonic batholiths. Sometimes when a planet's tectonic plates are thin enough and its molten subsurface hot enough, magma can force its way through the thin crust in serial piercings."

"Recent?"

"Hardly," said Joan as she gently paddled over the black hole of one of the cones, directing her personal light source into its inky depths. Jules watched her from his position at the hole's edge. Outlined in the greenish glow from the distant cage, he was still able to admire her graceful movements despite the EVA harness she wore.

"Jules, I think I saw something..." was all Jules had time to hear over his helmet speakers when he was thrown back by a sudden gust of pressure in the surrounding sea.

When he had recovered his balance, it was with Joan's screams in his ears. Kicking furiously, he pulled his way back up the steep slope of the cone coming back into the circle of dim light and almost tumbling down the other side into the hole. Overhead, where only seconds before, he had admired his wife's beauty, there was now the horror of ropy tentacles, thick as a bundle of straw, whipping and waving in blind groping, as if the creature that owned them had been surprised by Joan's beam of light. Jules recognized the thing as a bio-weapon employed by the Coalition. Able to operate in extreme environments including a vacuum, it had proved an effective defense against EVA mobilized boarding parties earlier in the war.

Forcing himself to remain calm, he searched the confusion of limbs for a sign of Joan, unconsciously taking his blaster in hand. Perspiration creeping down his forehead, he began making his way around the rim of the hole, Joan's screams still in his helmet's receivers.

"Joan. Joan, listen to me. I can't spot you. You have to get hold of yourself and help me find you."

He waited three endless seconds before he noticed her screams faded and her voice began to come over the communications link.

"Jules, Jules, hurry, it's all around me. I can't see where..."

There was silence then, and Jules could only wait and agonize on the fate of his wife when he heard the unmistakable click of the homing beacon being tongued on from her helmet. Suddenly, the head-up display just over his eyes gave him an exact fix on her position. Purpose giving his actions impetus, he made his way in as close as he could to where the beacon indicated Joan ought to be; she was still completely hidden from him by the cluster of tentacles. Using his pulse blaster as carefully as a surgeon might use a laser scalpel, he began to part the intervening limbs, opening a way to Joan. At last, a gasp of relief punctuated her pleas for haste.

"Jules, I can see you. I think the creature's grip is easing away."

"Can you get your blaster free?" asked Jules.

"I think so." A grunt. "I just have to squeeze past...I have it."

"Good, start helping yourself out."

Somewhat relieved, Jules risked taking his attention from Joan to look around for more of the creatures. There were none, or at least, none in sight.

"I can see you now, Joan," he said. "Now direct your fire at the body of the thing. That should stun it enough so that you can work your way free."

Following Jules' suggestion, Joan finally freed herself from the last ropy appendage and the two Terrans began to swim away from over the opening as quickly as they could. It wasn't fast enough as they suddenly found themselves being pursued by a trio of alien shapes.

"Jules," cried Joan, "those look like..."

"I know, Coalition troopers. We've got to get out of their reach as soon as possible."

"What are they doing here...?

"No time. Go ahead another hundred feet or so then turn around and cover me."

"What are you going to...?"

"Do as I say. I've seen these tactics before. They'll all come after me but when you're out of reach, turn around and lay a covering fire with your blaster."

As Joan pulled away, Jules turned and fired his own blaster without taking time to aim. He was lucky. The pulse tore away a connection to one of the aliens' pressure tanks, sending the thing into a panic. As it struggled to contain the leak, the other two fired at Jules with cold beam weapons that missed by a wide margin. Apparently, the two failed to take the effects of their environment into account. Keeping the lesson in mind, Jules took more careful aim this time and caught a second Coalition trooper square in its middle. Simultaneously, the third was struck just below its vestigial set of arms as Joan brought her own blaster to bear.

"Thanks, hon," gasped Jules, kicking out with a foot and sending the wounded trooper spinning head over feet. Not bothering with the niceties of the interstellar war council, he made sure the aliens would never pose a threat to them again by playing his blaster liberally over the bodies.

"I think they've had it," Jules heard Joan saying over his helmet receiver.

"Guess so," was all Jules could say.

"Was that how it really was on the front lines?" asked Joan.

"I thought you said there was no macro-life on this planet?" said Jules by way of reply. "How could you miss those troopers?"

"I don't understand, there wasn't supposed to be anything," said Joan, obviously confused. "Maybe something in the batholith formation's composition was able to mask the troopers' signature to our sensors."

"The batholiths themselves might be the source of the anomaly we came here to investigate."

"Possible. We'll have to get inside one of them to get some definitive answers."

"You're getting ahead of yourself, my dear," said Jules, chancing another look behind him. "Because if Pris and Finlay aren't tracking us topside—what the hell?"

Joan hesitated, slowed and turned cautiously. "What's the matter?"

"Depending on how you look at it, nothing. The troopers' bodies, they seem to have vanished."

"Vanished? No way they could move out of sight so fast in this medium."

"Where's the polymorph that attacked you? It's gone too. They all couldn't have just disappeared."

Joan shrugged, checking her sensor pad. "Nothing registering here."

"There wouldn't be if those batholiths really do have interference properties," said Jules, then "Hey, where are you going?"

"To check out the composition of that batholith," said Joan fearlessly. "Wherever the bodies went, I doubt if they could have drifted back inside before we could spot them."

"It sounds logical on the surface, but I wouldn't take it to the bank," said a wary Jules, moving quickly to catch up with her. "Hold it up a minute, Joan. Let me go first. There may be more troopers skulking around down there."

Using his thrusters at maximum, Jules soon caught up to his wife and signaling her back, drifted over the rim of the batholith. Carefully, he peeked inside but the darkness that gathered only a few feet down prevented him from seeing much.

"Well, it looks quiet at least. Hold off a minute while I bring in the cage."

A minute later, Jules directed the shuttle to take up a position directly over the batholith. The two divers watched as the glaring cage was again lowered to the opening in the strange formation.

"Let me ride the cage down first. If it's safe, I'll signal you to follow," said Jules.

"No argument," Joan replied.

Jules entered the cage and shut the gate. In seconds, he was being lowered past the rim of the opening into the murky interior of the batholith. He just had time to catch a glimpse of his rocky, striated surroundings when the cage lights went out...then on again...then out again. It wasn't a regular flicker but a more intermittent off and on effect. Sometimes the light would remain on for a few seconds, then a few minutes, creating a kind of off kilter strobe effect.

He checked the cage's status board and could learn nothing from its conflicting signals. That was one thing, but how to explain the fact that his own on-board instrument packages began to act up? Status lights began to flicker, digital readouts began to run on in endless streams of nonsensical data, range-finders and sensors went haywire. Jules, alarmed, stopped the cage, relieved that for the moment it still seemed to be functioning and motioned with his hand for his wife to hang back.

"What's wrong?" asked Joan from where she hovered a few feet above the rim of the batholith.

"I don't know for sure, but it looks like I've got a complete systems crash on my hands. How's your suit behaving?"

Joan ran a fast systems check. "Okay for the most part, but my environment indicator is acting a bit wonky."

"Hold back while I troubleshoot."

While he worked, he began to notice he didn't feel so good.

Feelings of nausea alternated with those of unaccountable weakness, pain in his joints and irregularity in his heartbeat. In the meantime, he had to admit defeat in trying to determine what was wrong with his instruments. As far as he could tell, they were fine when they weren't going haywire and when they *were* haywire, he couldn't do a thing to run a diagnostic.

"How are you doing?" asked Joan, her voice moving in and out over Jules' helmet receiver.

"Good question," Jules admitted. "There's definitely something down here that's interfering with our instruments, but without them, I can't identify it. Also, I'm starting to feel ill."

"Anything serious? Should we pull back?"

"No, not yet. I think we shouldn't stay in the cage, there's a chance we won't be able to get out if its systems fail too."

"What about sign of any more Coalition troopers?"

"Nothing yet."

"Then I'm coming down."

"Okay, but take it slow, honey."

Joan began to move toward the flashing glare of the suspended cage, the figure of her husband now visible, now hidden in darkness just outside its opened gate. As she neared him, not only did her own instruments begin to malfunction, but she began to experience the same physical symptoms as Jules.

"How are you feeling?" asked Jules when she reached his side.

"Weird, like my body doesn't know whether it has a cold, the flu, or malaria..." For a moment, she held a hand over her visor in an unconscious attempt to rub her head.

Jules held her by the shoulders and drew her close, tapping their helmets together. When Joan removed her hand from her visor, her face was hidden in darkness from the momentary failure of her interior instrument lights. The lights came back on and Jules had the shock of his life. Then, in a flash, what he thought he saw was gone.

The surprise and consternation must have been written on his face, because Joan, her eyes wide and riveted to his, asked, "Jules, what's wrong? Are you all right?"

Jules shook himself. "Yeah, yeah, I guess so...say, you'll never guess what I spotted on the bottom of this batholith."

Relieved to see Jules back to normal, Joan was eager to play along with his enthusiasm. "More aliens?"

"No, a spacecraft."

"Makes sense. Where else would those troopers have come from?"

"It must have crashed here somehow. It's hard to judge for sure in this on again, off again light, but it looks like a Coalition ship but of a design I've never seen before."

"A Coalition ship? Then it must be hiding here from their defeat at Procyon."

"I don't think it's hiding, although it's possible that may have been its original intention," said Jules. "From what I can see, it looks severely damaged. Ruptured hull, crushed bow. I think it was forced to make a crash landing here and sunk like a rock. Uhh..."

"What's wrong, darling?" said Joan, gripping Jules' arm in sudden desperation.

"Don't know, just another of the weird bodily effects this place is causing. Wish I could figure out why..." He stopped suddenly, looking intently at the shipwreck hundreds of feet below him. Straightening, he took hold of Joan, and again pressed his helmet to hers, again waited for the light inside her helmet to come on and allow him a good look at her face.

"What?" asked Joan worriedly.

Jules didn't answer but kept studying her instead. For a brief moment the same look of shock flickered across his face to be quickly replaced with a frown. The kind of frown Joan was used to seeing on him when he was concentrating on a particularly knotty problem.

He whirled suddenly, involuntarily moving in closer to the Coalition wreck below them.

"Well, I'll be damned..." he said at last.

"Jules, what's wrong?"

For a few more minutes, Jules remained silent then, turning slowly, said, "Joan, I think I've got the answer for what's happening to our instruments, to us, hell, to what's even been effecting the sensors of the *Burroughs* and military craft farther out in space. It's that ship down there." He took hold of Joan and directed her gaze at the spot where the Coalition craft lay. "Look closely at the area immediately surrounding it."

Joan, still holding her husband's arm, did so, but saw nothing.

"Look harder."

"There's some kind of shimmer..."

"Exactly. That distortion in the sea surrounding the ship is the only clue we have to what's causing all the trouble." He spun her around and tapped his helmet to hers. "Watch my face closely and tell me what you see."

For a few minutes, Joan's face remained blank then, eyes wide, recoiled and would have lost her equilibrium if Jules hadn't had a good hold on her. He drew her closer again until once more they could observe each other's faces. "Do you see what I'm talking about?"

"I--I don't know. I thought I saw you as an old man--I mean--the way you'd look if you were seventy or eighty years old! It must have been a trick of the light." Just the same, she resisted looking directly at his face again.

"No darling, it's not a trick of the light," said Jules. "The feelings of nausea and weakness we've been having are because our bodies have been shifting back and forth from youth to advanced age at a rapid rate. As a matter of fact, the shifts have been keeping almost regular time with the flickering of the cage lights and our suit systems. Joan, we're being shifted in time from the present to the past and to the future. When we're shifted to our future, aged selves we feel the symptoms of age; heart disease, arthritis, shortness of breath and when we shift to the past, our strength is renewed. The nausea comes in the moments of transition. Even our instruments, the cage, everything around us as a matter of fact, is caught up in the same phenomenon. That's why the lights keep flickering. They keep shifting from different points in their powered lives from high power reserves to low. And the gibberish our instruments keep reading isn't just nonsense, it's the readings for this place in different times, but because the changes come so fast, our instruments can't keep up with them."

"Jules, you're rambling," complained Joan, hardly able to keep up with her husband's speculations. "How can time be shifting like you say?"

Jules let her go and turned his body enough to throw his glance back down toward the wrecked spacecraft. He nodded inside his helmet.

"It's coming from that ship. I've seen something like this before. I think the Coalition have been secretly using some form of faster-than-light temporal technology to power their ships..."

"What kind of technology?"

"Temporal technology. A way to travel faster than the speed of light using time," said Jules. "The Consortium experimented with it years ago. The Coalition had it first and after managing to get our hands on some of it, we reverse engineered it. It showed promise but we were forced to discontinue the research when it became apparent there was no way to guarantee containment if there was an accident with the technology. After all, if it could be used, temporal technology would have been applied first to war craft, and during battle the likelihood of a hit striking the temporal equipment was way too high to risk."

"What would they be risking?"

"A rupture in time. No one knew exactly what that would mean, but there were theories: time could be bent, twisted, mixed, the immutable laws of nature would become elastic and unpredictable. It would make civilization itself an impossibility. Even individual human life would become unrecognizable as it was shifted from the past to the future at always alternating speeds. Just the effects we're experiencing right now."

"But...what's doing it?"

"I think the Coalition is using black hole technology. They've managed to somehow create...or trap...a temporal black hole and install it in their ships or at least in the one we have here. Maybe it was damaged in the action off Procyon, the protective casing used to contain the black hole was damaged and now the temporal distortion effects have become loosed. If they're not stopped, they'll keep spreading at a geometrical pace until they've encompassed the entire galaxy!"

"And it's this temporal black hole they've used to travel faster than light?"

"Right. It's a lot more efficient than your standard sub-photon drive the Consortium uses. Properly controlled, the temporal black hole can be made to fold time. In effect, transporting the ship that contains it from one place to another in no time at all. You can see the advantages such a system would have for any spacefaring civilization."

"According to reports, the action off Procyon began suddenly, when Coalition ships ambushed the fleet…"

"Now we know, it wasn't so much an ambush as the Coalition ships appearing instantaneously among the Consortium's and getting the drop on them. It was only because of the quality of their training that our sailors were able to keep their heads and turn the tables on the enemy."

"But Jules," said Joan, "if Coalition ships are using this technology, the authorities have to be warned. Any strike on an enemy ship could risk breaching a casing and loosing this same kind of danger."

"We'll warn them but right now, there's no time," shouted Jules through his balky helmet microphone. "Already the event horizon is moving outward; at the speed it's expanding, it'll engulf this whole planet in a few hours, after that, it'll be too late for anyone to do anything about it. By the time help can arrive here from Sol , the temporal effects will be pronounced so far beyond the planet's surface, they'll disrupt anyone trying to make an approach. On the other hand, there is one chance to stop it, but it might be dangerous…"

"For who? You? Jules, I won't…"

"It's our only chance, the only chance for the whole galaxy," said Jules desperately. "If I don't take this chance now, it'll be too late later."

"All right, all right, I guess I have no good argument against it if you feel it's that important." If Jules' guesses about the danger were right, then Joan could have no logical objection to his trying to end it except that she loved him and didn't want to see him dead. That was illogical, wasn't it? She had to keep telling herself that, otherwise she might pull her blaster and force him to come away with her. Instead, she said, "What can you do about it now? You can't put the genie back in the bottle."

"That's a good analogy Joan," said Jules, fighting a twinge of nausea. "In this case, the genie has peculiar qualities that might allow me to do just that."

"How?"

"Well, it's only theory of course," Jules admitted. "If my guess about this being a temporal black hole is right and if I can place myself at its core, I might be able to restore whatever containment mechanism its

Coalition designers had used to keep the time fluctuations in check."

"Those are a lot of ifs."

"Nevertheless, the more I think about it, the more I feel it can be done," said Jules, "providing I don't get caught in a time stream where I've died already..."

Joan's eyes grew big but Jules cut her off before she could say anything more.

"Just hold my legs as I reach out for the event horizon. There'll be some physical distortion as I move closer to the black hole, but don't worry, they'll be kind of like the distortion you see in an object lowered in the water. From my perspective beyond the horizon, I'll be perfectly normal. Ready?"

"What do you want me to do?"

"That's a brave girl. Let's move in a little closer."

They drifted downward a few dozen feet more until Joan could plainly see the distortion effect in the surrounding sea as it shifted from how it would be in the future to what it had been in the past.

"Anchor me here," said Jules as he stretched himself out.

Joan did as she was asked and watched in amazement as Jules' body seemed to stretch and lengthen toward the alien vessel. Soon it appeared to her that he must be hundreds of feet long, stretched taut like an elastic band ready to snap. She fought down an urge to panic, to yank him back, repeating to herself over and over again it was only a trick of the eyes...

Farther down, near the rocky, uneven floor of the batholith, Jules was making his approach to the downed spacecraft. As he swam closer, the alternating effects of the area's temporal flux became more pronounced. At times, he could hardly concentrate on what he was doing the pain was so great. He felt certain he was in a race not only against the rate of expansion of the event horizon, but of the rate of shift from his own past and future selves. If he didn't find a solution to the crisis fast, he'd be dead of old age. Nevertheless, he took the time for a quick glance back at Joan. His heart leapt, not with the effects of the black hole this time, and a lump rose unbidden in his throat. He could barely make her out beyond the event horizon, but his knowledge of her presence spurred him on to the task he had set himself.

His thoughts were interrupted by movement in the direction of the breach in the wreck's hull. There, three figures emerged followed by a ropy horror that quickly overtook and passed the others on its way out of the Batholith. It was the party of alien troopers on their way to attack him and Joan a few minutes before. They must have been survivors of the crash still bent on protecting their ship even at the cost of potential rescue. Trusting to the fact the troopers had already been successfully taken care of, Jules ignored the time anomaly and continued his downward course.

Now the Coalition craft loomed above him as he swam in close. He passed the ruined bow where the ship's crew would normally have stayed and continued on to the gaping slash in its rear portion. Careful to avoid snagging his EVA suit on the ragged edges of the ruptured hull, Jules slipped into the darkened interior. Inside, in the strobe-flicker of his personal light source, he could make out the tangled remains of the ship's propulsion system. Vast conduits and thick, ropy cables twisted off into the gloom in either direction. Recognizing the conventional configurations of standard sub-photon drive engines, he ignored them and moved deeper into the ship's insides.

Presently, he came upon the expected photon shifters and beyond them the glare of the singularity. He hadn't known quite what to expect when he finally came into the direct presence of a temporal black hole, but somehow the glaring white, the absolute absence of not only color, but shadow and substance, texture and even place did not surprise him. He moved forward, slow, not with hesitancy but with careful appreciation for the marvel he found himself suddenly a part of. Terror then slipped from him, replaced with awe and wonder and curiosity. Time continued to fracture, but with such a rapid pace that it ceased to be differentiated as past, present, future. Now it was all one. A smile of delight came unbidden to his lips. Then he laughed. Not with madness but with sudden knowledge and appreciation. How simple it all seemed now/then. His body had ceased to give him trouble. He felt the best he ever had/did. In a moment of severe clarity, he knew how it felt to be God...to be able to see the past, present, future all at the same time. To see every choice, every random event, and all their attendant effects on the time stream. It was like a vast pool constantly aflicker, ashimmer with change. Oh, how wonderful it all was.

Amid that transcendent feeling, he seemed to remember another life and another soul. Dimly at first, then more strongly, he recalled—Joan. He at last remembered he was but a man after all.

Outside, in the glare of Procyon A the brighter, main sequence star of the system's binary arrangement, the navies of two warring interstellar leagues crashed in an unplanned encounter. Molecular borers and photon pulse guns exchanged fire as the Consortium's ships managed to evade direct hits. Luck was with them as their own return fire struck home again and again forcing the Coalition vessels to fall back around the white dwarf of Procyon B. Among the retreating vessels was that upon which Jules labored in the black hole containment chamber.

Focusing all the consciousness he could, he forced the infinity of happenings, occurrences, possibilities aside. He threaded his way past the surface of the shimmering lake to the underlying fabric. He found the human texture of its strands and thrust apart the individual events of a universe of chance until at last, he arrived in the here and the now. He remembered the reason he came, shifted a bit this way then a bit that way and found what he was looking for.

Suddenly, a loud booming rang through the ship followed by a lurch that forced him to concentrate on retaining his balance for a moment. Steadying himself, he looked around and suddenly, he was back in Joan's arms.

"What...happened?" was all she could muster.

The last she remembered was holding onto Jules for dear life. Then, she experienced some kind of instinctual understanding and she threw her arms around his neck. The embrace was awkward in the EVA harnesses and bulky helmets, but the emotions exchanged were nonetheless real. After a few moments, they came apart.

"I fixed it," said Jules finally.

"The containment unit for the black hole?"

"Right. Oh, I guess I could've fixed it so the hull rupture had never occurred, but then that would've left us aboard a Coalition war craft with no explanation of why we were aboard, let alone while wearing EVA harnesses. Instead, I got the idea of restoring the containment unit only a few minutes before I dove down to fix it in the first place. This way, the ship stays here as proof of the technology's danger and allows the Consortium to negotiate with the Coalition to refrain from using such technology. Hopefully, the enemy will come to realize not using it is to their advantage as well as ours."

"How did you do it? Contain the black hole that is."

"Oh that." Jules shrugged. "I'll admit those Coalition scientists were ingenious in finding a way to contain and at the same time harness for use a temporal black hole. They built a radical cube then grew the temporal black hole inside it. It must have been a long process so my hope is that this ship and the handful of others that appeared off Procyon were actually only a few working models. It'll make stopping the use of such technology so much easier."

"You're getting ahead of me, Jules. What's a radical cube?"

"A concept we've known about for a while but never dared build. A radical cube exists in four dimensions at the same time, height, width, depth and time. It's the last quality that makes it perfect for containing a temporal black hole. The only problem is, the part of it that exists in time is the easiest part to disrupt. That was the part that gave in when the ship was struck, releasing the time distortion effects of the black hole. What I did was to go to the moment just before the ship was hit off Procyon, dismantle the cube myself, take it with me to a point in time just before I began my descent over the event horizon and rebuild it around the black hole. That way, time wasn't changed, the effects of the black hole were still released during the battle, but this time not as a result of battle, but because I had dismantled the cube. The resultant time distortions affected the crew enough to make them once again crash land here thus allowing us to do again what we had done in the previous reality. Get it?"

Joan shook her head. "No, but just so long as you're safe."

They held hands then and didn't let go until the cage had deposited them back on the shuttle.

There were some things, however, that Jules would never tell Joan about his experiences within the time flux, but unknown to him, there was nothing more she needed to hear from him that she did not learn in the many secret lovers' embraces they would share in the years to come.

About the Author

Pierre V. Comtois has been the editor and publisher of *Fungi, the Magazine of Fantasy and Weird Fiction* since 1984 and has had a number of books released by numerous publishers including *Goat Mother and Others* by Chaosium Fiction in 2015, *A Well Ordered Universe* by Desert Breeze Publishers in 2016, and *Marvel Comics in the 1980s: An Issue by Issue Field Guide to a Pop Culture Phenomenon* by Twomorrows Pubs in 2015. More recent releases include *Scheduled for Extinction*, a science fiction novel from Desert Breeze and *Talismanic,* a horror novel from Rogue Phoenix Press. Comtois has contributed fiction to many small press magazines over the years including various Chaosium Books anthologies. The author has also written a number of other books including novels such as *Strange Company* and *Sometimes a Warm Rain Falls*; non-fiction such as *Our Lives, Our Fortunes, Our Sacred Honor*; and short story collections such as *The Way the Future Was* and *The Portable Pierre V. Comtois*. Comtois has also found the time to contribute non-fiction articles to such magazines as *World War II, America's Civil War, Wild West,* and *Military History*, many of which were collected in *Hazardous History*. For more information visit www.pierrevcomtois.com.

Also by the Author
at
Rogue Phoenix Press

Talismanic

Glenn Springer could hardly believe his good luck. After moving to Maine to escape the Boston rat race, he bought a farm, was successful, and became the envy of his neighbors. Then, he fell in love with the beautiful and bewitching Grizelle Beaumarchais. Was his good fortune all due to a locket he found inside the walls of his old farmhouse? And why was Grizelle so interested in it? Could it have anything to do with her being descended from an Indian shaman? Why were there things about herself that Grizelle wasn't telling him? Was his love for her genuine or was he being subtly manipulated? His luck, it seemed, had its price, and as Glenn began to realize, the bill was coming due.

Prologue

Hugging his muzzle-loading, long rifle close to his chest, Nathanael Winsor walked through the misty Maine woods with a number of his fellows detached from General Benedict Arnold's army that was headed north to invade Canada.

A Groton resident, he'd arrived too late to help out against the British troops that retreated from Concord earlier in the year, but earned his veteran's status at the Battle of Breed's Hill. Afterward, he'd discovered he had a taste for battle and when Arnold asked for volunteers to accompany him on a bold move to capture Canada from the British, he fancied the adventure.

Unfortunately, adventure took a back seat in the buggy to the sheer drudgery of marching through unmarked wilderness and the onset of winter. That had been bad enough, but poor planning and inexperience made things worse. First, the boats used to get the army up the Kennebec River leaked, spoiling both gunpowder and food supplies. As cold weather set in the men began to go hungry and many turned back. Maybe he should have too, but Nathanael always had a stubborn streak and once he'd set his mind on something, it was seldom he changed it.

Not that he didn't have second thoughts at times. Just now, for instance, with his stomach growling, he couldn't decide which was worse, hunger or the constant, discomforting cold.

To add to his misery, a light snow fell during the night, crusting the surface of the ground in patches of white. Feet crunching as he walked, Natty reached a big tree and took a moment to rest against it.

Behind him, the rest of the hunting party caught up. There were a dozen of them, chosen, like himself, because they were all good shots, to range afield in search of game which was desperately needed to feed Arnold's dwindling army and fuel its passage over the final leg of the march to the Chaudiere River.

They had left the army a few days before as it huddled around its meagre campfires and moved up along the Kennebec. One good thing about the snowfall, it made tracking game easier and signs had pointed away from the river. Wary of local Indians, the hunting party spread out along the trail with Natty in the lead. Now, pausing behind the tree, he watched the others as they drew up to him.

"Find anything, Natty?" asked Homer Lawton, a volunteer from Pepperell.

"Just resting a bit, but it can't be long now."

"Sure is cold," said Homer, his breath steaming on the frigid air.

Nathanael didn't reply.

"All right," he said finally, as the rest of the party gathered around the tree. "We must be close now. Spread out and let's see if we can flush something out."

Slowly, the ragged figures moved off to left and right of the tree and when all were in a rough line, Nathanael stepped out and led the way forward.

As he walked, Nathanael could not help noticing how quiet the forest was. All around him, leafless, lifeless trees stood motionless and overhead a slate grey sky hung featureless and lowering. Along the ground, the morning mist still clung, revealing the game trail only a few feet at a time.

Suddenly, Nathanael stopped.

The deer sign they had been following was still present, but now there were other prints, human prints.

"Hold it," he whispered; a command that was passed along the line of men to the right and left.

Pointing, Nathanael signaled danger ahead. The others understood. They'd wait and follow his lead in silence.

Warily he continued, until a shot rang out.

Instantly, Nathanael threw himself to the ground as did many of the others. Some scooted behind nearby trees. But nothing else happened. There were no other shots. Maybe it was not aimed at them? If so, the hunting party had not been discovered. It still held the element of surprise.

Cautiously, Nathanael regained his feet and moved slowly forward, followed by the others. Soon, shapes began to take form in the mist, shapes he recognized as the kind of temporary structures used by Indians. Instantly, he halted and waved his fellows in.

With furtive movements, they drew themselves together until the entire band crouched among a stand of white pine.

"What do we do now?" asked someone.

"They must know we're here."

"Don't look like it to me…"

"What about that shot?"

"Hold on," said Nathanael. "There's nothing to suggest they were shooting at us. Otherwise, there would have been more."

"Natty's right," began Homer before being interrupted by a second shot, this one no doubt aimed at them as a ball shredded its way through the clustered pine branches overhead.

"Quick, spread out and return fire," advised Nathanael as he unlimbered his own rifle and took aim at a figure standing amid the bark structures.

Boom! His gun unloaded and for a few seconds there was too much powder smoke to tell if he'd hit his target.

When the smoke cleared, however, he had the satisfaction of seeing the figure lying in a crumpled heap on the frozen ground. By then, the air was filled with the loud retorts of other guns as the hunting party fired on the village. With a shout, the little band of soldiers advanced, some stopping to reload their muskets and firing again.

To add to the confusion, some of the men set fire to the lodges whose bark walls and thatched roofs went up quickly.

Nathanael was reloading his rifle when he spotted the Indian sitting at a campfire at the edge of the village. Throughout all the noise, commotion and flying balls, he continued to sit, smoking a long-stemmed pipe just as if nothing was happening.

Suddenly, determined to shatter the old man's tranquility and to see him hop to his feet in alarm, Natty aimed his rifle and shot. The old man didn't move. Still he sat there smoking. Unsure of how he'd missed, Natty loaded again, took more careful aim, this time squarely at the old man's form and fired.

Again, he'd apparently missed. Impossible. He knew he was a darn good shot, could shoot the eye out of a running squirrel at a hundred yards. Something was not quite right…but just then Homer appeared, urging him to signal the retreat.

"Let's get out of here," said Homer. "The boys don't like the way the Injuns all scattered. Likely the rascals are somewhere and figurin' on comin' back and catchin' us unawares."

Nathanael's back was up however. All he wanted to do right then was to stomp up to the old man and put a bullet in him.

"What are we waitin' fer?" asked someone else. "We don't want to be caught in some ambush so far from the rest of the army."

Clearly, the boys were spooked at the sudden encounter with the Indians and Nathanael felt the pressure to turn back.

"All right, let's go," he said at last.

A few minutes later, he found himself hanging back as the rest of the party headed back the way they'd come. A sense of unfinished business teasing at his mind, Natty couldn't go on until he settled affairs with the old Indian.

As the last man passed him, he turned and faded into the mist. A few minutes later, he'd returned to the village which by that time was only a collection of smoking ruins. The inhabitants still hadn't come back. Likely they were as shaken as his men had been and were miles away by now.

Slowly, he crept from tree to tree until coming in sight of the old man's lodge. The only one unharmed by the recent action despite being near the center of the village. The coincidence only added to Nathanael's curiosity as he watched the old Indian, still sitting by his fire.

Suddenly, he stood and entered his dwelling.

On impulse, Nathanael stole from cover and dashed to the lodge. Entering, he cornered the old man before he had a chance to do anything.

"Welcome young warrior," said the Indian, startling Nathanael.

"You speak English?"

"Yes. I learned it many years ago when the first wooden villages came to fish off of these shores. In those days, none of my people had ever seen a white man and we were very curious about them. I was young then myself and being bolder than most, I clambered aboard one of the ships when invited and was taken to England. There, I learned your language."

Nervous, Nathanael looked around quickly before replying.

"You're talking a hundred, two hundred years ago, old man."

"Longer."

"What...?" Nathanael managed, confused.

"It does not matter. I know why you have come." The old man fingered a small metal locket that hung around his neck. "You cannot put it into words, but you wondered why I was not harmed when you shot at me before. It is because of this." He lifted the locket away from his chest. "I obtained it in England long ago. It contains a gift from Wahn-di-ko that has given me favor for many years, but now I am tired of it. I have lived for too many years. That is why I am prepared to make a trade with you."

"A trade?"

"I give you the gift and in return, you kill me with your musket. In the heart. Do not miss."

"You want me to kill you?"

"Is that so hard? You are a warrior. You have killed before. Even now you go with many of your fellows north to kill again. What is one old Indian?"

At that, the old man lifted the locket from around his neck and presented it to Nathanael.

"Keep it with you always. With it, you will never come to harm. With Wahn-di-ko's favor, you will prosper."

Nathanael took the locket and clutched it tightly in his fist.

The old man stood back and pulled his thin shirt open, exposing his chest.

"Now, kill me!"

Almost without volition, Nathanael found himself tucking the locket into a pocket and raising his musket. He hesitated a moment and wondered if it was his imagination or if the old man's skin was really wrinkling before his eyes, spotting up, turning a pale waxy yellow...

Boom!

Nathanael pulled the trigger and the blast of his gun sounded like a cannon inside the walls of the lodge. Wondering if what he'd seen had been his imagination, he waited for the powder smoke to clear to make sure of his kill.

The old Indian lay there, his chest a bloody mess, but a smile nevertheless teased the corners of his mouth, an ironic smile it seemed to Nathanael who retreated from the lodge. Not waiting to reload his rifle, he quickly stole back into the surrounding forest, suddenly eager to catch up with the rest of his comrades.

Chapter One

Best Laid Plans

"A chicken farm?"

Glenn Springer still recalled the incredulity with which his revelation had been received by Paul Roundhouse, the chief accountant at Silver and Sax where he also worked as office manager.

He smiled at the recollection, especially juxtaposed against the high rises of downtown Boston that formed the backdrop to the thirty sixth floor office space rented by the firm in the John Hancock Tower.

It wasn't the kind of thing that often came up for conversation in such an environment, but it was one ventured by Springer when he sought some unofficial counsel from Roundhouse.

"A chicken farm?" Roundhouse asked again after nearly spurting out the mouthful of coffee he'd sipped just after Glenn mentioned his plans. "You mean, like roosters and clucking hens and heads being chopped off?"

Glenn laughed. "Well not the head chopping part, anyway. It's not that kind of farm."

"What then?"

"Eggs. It raises eggs for market in supermarkets and stuff like that."

"Eggs, heads, what's the difference? A farm is a farm in a nowhere backwater. Why are you even thinking of burying yourself out in Hicksville anyway?"

"It's not Hicksville," said Glenn defensively. "It's Bingham, Maine."

"Whatever. You mean you're serious about this? You want to buy a chicken farm?"

"I've been thinking about it for a long time. Well, about buying a farm anyway. But a chicken farm raising eggs is even better. Less labor intensive."

"But still, isn't that a little drastic just to get some fresh air? Why not just plant a garden in your backyard?"

"Hard to do that when I live in a condo in Lowell."

It would be even harder when he spent hours every day making the commute from Boston to his condo located in a restored mill building.

Renovating nineteenth century mill buildings was all the rage at the moment, especially in Lowell where such buildings stood empty and crumbling for decades before the federal government began pouring in urban renewal and national park funding into them. Now they were mostly high-end condominiums that had proven attractive to up and coming professionals who found the rents and real estate values in Boston not worth the quality of life involved.

Lowell offered the sophistication of an urban environment without the close quarters or crime levels of the big city. It was an easy commute from Boston. Well, it was supposed to be. Only forty-five minutes on a good day, more often work days meant an hour and a half at best.

Just now, Glenn was being reminded of why he'd finally decided to take the plunge into something he always thought of doing. Namely, moving away from the city completely for the wide-open spaces and slower pace of rural life. It was something that buoyed his spirits as he sat at a dead stop in the center of I-93, a four-lane interstate highway that ran straight as an arrow northwest from Boston to New Hampshire and points beyond.

Glenn eased the brake a little and inched up a few feet before being forced to stop by the endless line of cars that stretched farther than his eye could see. Likely there was an accident ahead that everyone had to slow down to look at, thus backing up traffic for miles.

It merely served to remind him of why he hated this commute. Forcing himself to be patient, he selected the classical music station on the radio and relaxed a little, telling himself things would soon be better. In his mind, he saw again the rambling forests of upstate Maine punctuated now and then by fields of produce arranged in geometric perfection. Potato fields mostly, he guessed, but plenty of corn too. By now the ears must be fat and ready for picking. A thousand roadside vegetable stands would be bursting with baskets of the stuff and streams of seasonal sightseers from Massachusetts buying it up for pots back home.

He wouldn't be one of them.

He pictured the farmhouse on the property that soon would be his. The several outbuildings and large coops filled with squawking hens and raucous roosters. Nothing to do but get up early in the morning and collect the night's eggs. Supervise the packing and meeting the truckers coming in to haul the eggs to warehouse distribution centers in Massachusetts. In the evening, relaxing by the fire and doing a little reading and bookkeeping until bedtime.

Glenn was imagining how good a night's sleep would be after days like that, out in the fresh air...

A horn blasted almost right alongside him, but traffic was still not going anywhere. *Jerk.*

Shifting mental gears, Glenn again recalled his conversation with Paul earlier that day. He'd had a bookkeeping question he wanted to run past him and couldn't do it without telling him about his plans.

"Seriously? A chicken farm?" Paul asked.

"Seriously. I always like the outdoors, doing work outdoors like raking leaves in the fall or mowing the lawn in the summer, going in the woods to look for saplings I could transplant to my yard. Stuff like that. I still think plenty of fresh air is the key to health. Spending all day in an office like this, breathing in that recirculated, climate-controlled air can't be good for you."

"Yeah, I've read those articles too. But why an egg farm?"

"Why not? I wanted to get a place where I could make a living, at least a modest one. Like I said, straight vegetable farming is labor intensive. Something I don't think I want to tackle at my age. But a chicken farm, especially one that was already established and had steady customers for its eggs, I could handle that. So, I looked around, checked the internet, visited a couple places, until I found a place outside Bingham."

"You already went up to look at it?"

Glenn nodded. "Yup. It's about a fifteen-hour drive from Lowell. Pretty rural. Farm country for sure, but really attractive countryside. So, I put down a security deposit and expect to close in a couple months."

"That soon?"

"You're welcome to come up and check it out after the sale."

"I just might take you up on that, Glenn. I don't know any farmers."

"Anyway, just wanted to ask you about balance sheets, liability, accounts payable and receivable, and payroll."

"Anybody but yourself on that payroll?"

"Well, I'll have a few people working to pack the eggs and, for now, there's going to be a local farmer I'm going to let work some of my fields. We're going to split the profits from whatever he grows on them."

"That'll complicate your record keeping a little but no biggie."

"Taxes?" asked Glenn with some trepidation.

"Right."

By that point, break time was about over and he and Paul made arrangements to get together soon at the local Starbucks to go over the accounting issues in detail. In the meantime, Glenn asked Paul to keep the chicken farm deal under his hat.

Be that as it may, news about his impending plans leaked out to the rest of the office and for the last few weeks, he'd been the target of some good-natured ribbing, even from Robbie Sax himself. Glenn just hoped Paul was better at keeping professional secrets than he was about chicken farms.

Suddenly, there was a break ahead and traffic began moving more steadily.

If he was lucky, he might make it home before dark.